CHOOSING THE NEXT ME

Chuck First

This book is dedicated to my wife and children. They may be happy to know that no characters in this book are derived from my experiences with them. I leave that to their friends to write later.

CONTENTS

PREFACE

I decided to be an architect when I was in high school. Its greatest appeal was the fact it required creativity in two ways, as an art and a science. Those qualities are what attracted many in my generation into the field as well.

In the decades that followed, computer science offered alternatives that competed with traditional fine arts for those wishing to exercise their creative talents. Computer animation, web design and gaming graphics were new frontiers that lured younger generations away from the otherwise static fields of sculpture, painting and architecture.

This evolution penetrated into other fields, and coupled with far reaching developments in our society, now present unprecedented freedom in making life choices. Despite major swings in the economy, many people today can decide where they live, what work they do and who they live with.

As these options continue to multiply, the objects of our creativity may grow beyond our external world to include ourselves. As we redesign our environments, we will also redesign ourselves.

The stories that follow explore how and why five individuals embark on changes to themselves. Each in their own way, for reasons they consciously determine, end up -- choosing the NEXT me.

GOING TO MARKET

The secret of life is to validate your existence.

CARLOS SANTANA

He pulled onto a side street and found a half empty rack in which to park. Portland, Oregon being a bike friendly city, gave him plenty of places to select. He had just pedaled across the Burnside bridge from the Kern area, so he rested a second to catch his breath.

Timothy Rancini came over to the west side every Saturday. It was his favorite day of the week, and he especially enjoyed engaging with new people each time, locals and tourists alike. As he headed down the main street a young couple with a little girl and stroller approached from the opposite direction. The child pointed at him, looked up at her father, and unabashedly shouted, "Daddy, who is that strange man? He looks like a bear."

If Portland is anything, it is a refuge for diversity. Eccentricity is the norm. So his long flowing layered habit usually went unnoticed. It was unsurprising for a young child on the other hand to confuse the dark brown colored robes for a big lumbering mammal.

The mother flushed red with embarrassment. The father quickly interceded, "I'm very sorry. It's our first time here." then to the child, "This is a nice man, honey. He is a monk, not a bear."

"Whatza a monk?" she asked, still puzzled.

Timothy recognized that this was the type of question young children instinctively asked that silenced adults. Timothy knelt down to speak to the little girl, who stood her ground.

"Does your mom and dad talk to you about being good?" She nodded yes, timidly. "Well, a monk is someone who talks to adults, like your mom and dad, about being good. You look like you're a good young lady, so you deserve a little reward." He reached under his robe, pulled out a yo-yo, then looked to her parents who nodded ok before handing it to her.

"Keep on being a good young lady and listen to your mom and dad." The baby in the stroller started to fuss so Timothy stood up and said to the couple, "Your little one wants to keep moving. Have a blessed day. You have a beautiful family."

"Thanks," said the father and they each continued

on.

Not much further on his trek down Burnside was his usual first stop, a coffee shop called On What Grounds? When Timothy entered he picked up a free community paper from the rack. Corey DiBolo, the owner, saw him and came running over from behind the counter.

"Friar Luck, glad to see you. And how are you today?" Corey asked. He held the notion that having a man of the cloth somehow added credibility to his establishment and maybe even increased his odds for success, hence the nickname Friar Luck he bestowed on Timothy.

"Always glad to be here."

Corey waved his arm back toward the space and asked, "And what is your preference today?"

"Marlborough Lites."

Corey gave him an odd look, then realized the joke. "Always the comedian."

"One small way to bring happiness. That empty booth in the middle is fine. The usual bagel and coffee, please." The booth on the end was occupied by four die-hard long distance bikers all dressed in the same brightly colored spandex and helmets. Their loud chatter made the booth he chose attractive for reading. He looked over the schedule in the paper of upcoming events for the next month. An international festival was going to be held at the Lloyd Center next weekend. He might just break his routine and go there instead.

Corey returned with the order. Instead of leaving,

he slid into the seat across from Timothy. On the surface, he looked as if he should be bartending in a dive down by the docks, surrounded by Harley's. His head was clean shaven and his black t-shirt was stretched taut over a muscular core.

"Brother Timothy. I wonder if I could ask you something of a personal nature?"

"Of course you can. I'm always available for you," he reassured.

"My Dad down in Ogden is real sick. He was something of a heavy drinker. Has advanced cirrhosis of the liver and probably won't make it. He and I were always close. He's the one who helped me finance this place."

Timothy listened intently while Corey gave evidence of the bond that had fused over the years with his father.

"At this point he would need a miracle to stay with us. I thought that might be down your alley."

Without saying a word, Timothy reached across the table and took both of Corey's hands in his. He bowed his head in silence toward the table then Corey did the same. They sat quietly for a good five minutes despite the chatter from the back of the room.

When they both looked up, Corey wiped his eyes and was about to say something when Timothy pointed toward the front door. A short line had formed. Corey thanked Timothy profusely and got up to seat his customers. Timothy finished his bagel and coffee then left and continued his way along

Burnside. The morning was still young, and he already felt a sense of gratitude for having helped someone.

A brisk short walk brought him to the downtown market.

There are places in America that are living time capsules of decades past. They are populated by people who became one with their times, forever perpetuating the culture of that particular point in history. Martindale, Indiana preserved life of the 50's and Chester City, New Jersey the 40's. In this case, the Saturday Market was a refuge for the living 60's. The music, the language, the dress and most of all, the values were religiously preserved here.

Timothy walked among the booths and stands that were hawking arts dominated by tie-dye shirts, beads, psychedelic dresses, wood carvings and surreal paintings. Music abounded. Down one row, a banjo player plucked away at lightning speed. Down another, a man and woman sang mountain music with acoustic guitars in hand. A portable stage at the far end of the market was the source of thumping acid rock sounds.

Also scattered around was a wide variety of vegetarian snacks roasting on smoky grilles, scenting the air with an irresistible invitation to eat. Had Timothy not just downed a bagel, he would have been tempted to buy a bean taco. He just wandered along, not looking for anything in particular since much of the same stock of goods showed up each week. The draw was the vendors he had come to know since he was a regular fixture here.

As he stopped to scan a gallery of photographs featuring the Portland skyline, a female voice shouted from behind, "Father Tim, over here."

Recognizing the raspy voice, he turned and walked over to Zola Nebula's stall. She came around and hugged him the best she could considering his rotund bulk. Zola had a stocky but not muscular build sheathed within a rainbow colored muumuu. Her straw hat matched her straw colored fly away hair, some of which was bundled into a pony tail. Her skin was ruddy and wrinkled, a byproduct of years of smoking. Born and raised in a commune, she was unclear where her parents were originally from since they eventually split and went their separate ways. Zola Nebula wasn't her real name, but one she adopted to fit the New Age mentality at the time.

"I'm so glad you came today."

"Anything new today?" he asked. Zola's specialty was the peace symbol. She found ways to work it into almost anything. Her booth was a potpourri of items - lamp shades, cuff links, etchings, sun catchers and more. She was able to take the geometric shape of the symbol, multiply it and blend them together into intricate patterns resembling Persian tapestries.

"I recently started experimenting with mixing motifs. I'm not happy with the result so far, but you can have a look," she said while pulling out a tray from under the folding table.

He leaned over and studied them intently. There were broaches and necklaces made of polished walnut with conjoined heart and peace symbols intricately engraved across the surface.

"I'll take this one." he said, lifting his selection up by its leather lanyard strap. "I like it. It is interesting. How much?"

"You can have it. I wouldn't think of charging for such a raw piece of work."

"Nonsense. I can see you spent time on this. And it has a character that is unique." He then reached into his habit, and produced a pouch that gave him a ten-dollar bill.

"Thanks. I really shouldn't take this." But she did. "That little token doesn't begin to cover what I owe you. I got some news I have to tell you about. Come sit a moment."

Timothy squeezed between the two display tables and sat on an upended wooden crate. Zola ignored the other browsers at the table and continued.

"You'll never guess. I heard from my daughter last week."

"Zola, I didn't know you had a daughter!" he reacted in surprise.

"One child. Another product of the commune. After the group broke apart, so did my husband and I. He grew up, but I guess I didn't, so he got custody. Never saw or spoke to her since."

"So what brought this about?"

"Her name was Beverly, but I called her Cicada, because she was noisy at night. She turned 21 earlier this year and decided to seek me out, despite her father's objections. You can find almost anyone on the internet these days, and there aren't too many Zola Nebulas out there."

"That's wonderful! So what is my connection to this turn of events?"

"Remember last year when I got treatment for my addiction? I was at a low point in my life. It was you who prodded me to go to the rehab clinic. The crazy thing it was only a few blocks from here, but I could never get the money to go. I needed someone who cared enough to encourage me to get help. That was you."

"Thank you. You can be proud of what you accomplished. It took a lot of grit on your part to complete the program."

"Well, you got me going down the right path. Because of that I can see Cicada while I'm clean. Otherwise I might not have a chance to get back into her life. What you did for me was a blessing."

"This little peace and heart medallion takes on special meaning then," he said as he slipped the lanyard around his broad neck.

"Ma'am, would you be willing to take $15. for this mirror?" A tall lanky red headed man was holding the item. His offering was the opening volley for the bartering that was customary at Saturday market, at least among locals. Zola stood up to continue the counter offer routine.

"See you later," Timothy said as he squeezed back out onto the main aisle.

Meandering his way from booth to booth, he continued to chat with the craftsmen and admire their handiwork. It wasn't noon yet, but the smells from the concession stands overtook him. Despite knowing he should watch his weight, he broke down and bought a loaded coney dog and fries anyway.

At the rear of the grounds beside a large play area, he found an empty bench where he could be entertained by the children while he ate. Some played on the swings and slides, but most just ran and ran. Some chasing after one another, others by themselves for the sheer joy of movement. Timothy reflected on the fact that science was never able to invent a perpetual motion machine, yet here it was in abundance.

A man in a wheel chair was playing a harmonica several yards away. Half a dozen boys and girls sat on the ground in front of him entranced by the rapid fire stream of West Virginia melodies. He had seen Timothy's arrival, so when he finished, he had his aide roll him over to Timothy's bench. Albert Neen was another Saturday regular. The buttons and patches covering his black leather vest and cap advertised that he was a Vietnam vet. Several chains of dog tags hanging from his neck clattered as he moved.

"Well if it isn't the spunky monk. Glad to see you're here on schedule," Albert said, looking at his watch. They often met up with each other around this time, but Timothy hadn't seen him for recent weeks.

"Spunky is a bit of a stretch. I see you have a new helper with you."

"Yes. I'd like you to meet her." Alan looked up and back and pointed. "This is Mai Nguyen." He said a few words to her in Vietnamese. She stepped to the side, gave a quick nervous smile, and bowed her head.

"I went back to Vietnam for a month. Went with a group out of LA that specializes in tours there every year. It was great! We went through villages I was in during the war. Some of my buddies had gone before and it helped them work through some of their issues. The group found Mai and arranged for her to get me around. Something clicked and I talked her into coming back and moving in with me. I know it don't look proper from the way you look at things, but we're planning to get married. I was kind of hoping you'd see it clear to marry us -- make us legit."

"That's wonderful! Glad to see you found someone. You won't hear me disapproving of love. I'm flattered you want me to officiate your bond, but there are brethren better suited to do this."

"Aw, really. I'm disappointed. Are you sure you can't swing it?" he said tugging on Timothy's sleeve.

"Really. You deserve someone who can do it justice for you"

"Alright then. But at least I want you there for my hitching."

"Count on it. I wouldn't miss it for the world."

After filling in more details of his trip, Albert went back to entertaining the children, and Timothy continued to explore the remaining booths. He finished by early afternoon, then as was his usual practice, strolled over to Pioneer Square to enjoy the fountain and watch the people. His favorite seafood restaurant there provided an early dinner. From there he walked back toward the river, retrieved his bike and rode across the bridge back to Kern.

Rancini Aqua Mart, known within the trade as RAM, was both a consumer and contractor parts supplier for all things plumbing. Located not far from the Lloyd Center, it was an ok commute from Kern. Timothy rode the bike in on good days of which Portland had many.

As he coasted into the entrance drive, a small BMW convertible with its top down, music blaring, raced passed, nearly edging him into the drainage swale bordering the lot. After the car came to a screeching stop at the front door, Timothy's step brother Martyn Rancini jumped out of the car and quickly entered the building without acknowledging the close call.

Timothy continued around the back to the warehouse wing and storage yard, parking his bike, and entering through the double door at the loading dock. Two pack trucks were being loaded with deliveries. Several men on the platform were either pushing product on dollies or debating the best routes to run. All were too busy to take notice of him.

In the locker room he changed into the regulation gray uniform with the Aqua Mart logo. Last to go on were safety glasses and a bright yellow safety vest.

It didn't close completely shut due to his wide girth, but the order he placed for a larger one never seemed to get processed.

He then moved to the staging room that connected the warehouse with the sales floor. A set of wire basket racks were mounted on the wall beside the conference room. It was here he retrieved a stack of handwritten orders that were to be pulled and packed for delivery the next day. The company had not automated the procuring process like many of their competitors. There was a minor building boom underway in the region, mainly from California expatriates migrating to Oregon, and since they were successful without the investment, there was no incentive to change. For a family owned business, this meant more profit for the owners.

Julian Rancini abruptly entered the room from the dock. Julian was Timothy's other step-brother and preferred parking by the dock. Being sales manager he came and went frequently and vacant spaces were more likely to be open in the back. In fact, both step-brothers were managers reporting directly to their father, Avery.

Rushing passed Timothy without greeting, Julian stopped and turned as if suddenly remembering something.

"Where were you Saturday?"

"Out."

"We tried calling you. Got no answer."

"Left my cell at home. Easier to focus on other stuff."

"Well we had a big rush order come in over the weekend. Needed 30 orders pulled. Just like always, we can't count on you in the crunch."

"There are other order pullers. Jeff and Larry. They could have come in."

"We would have had to pay them overtime. You need to carry your cell so you're available. I'm going to bring this up with Mr. Rancini."

"You mean Dad?"

Julian just stood, his face turning red at the distasteful reminder that they were related.

Martyn poked his head out the conference room door. "Julian, get over here! We're starting the meeting."

Julian went over to join the group while glaring back at Timothy.

With orders in hand, Timothy found his pushcart, went back into warehouse and descended into the realm of copper and plastic elbows, valves and gauges.

Ever since his father and mother divorced, he had been distanced from the family. It was understandable that Julian and Martyn would be the focus of Avery's attention. They were the ones who went to business school and probably would inherit Aqua Mart. The one token of family loyalty Avery showed for Timothy was to give him this job.

No matter. As menial and boring as it was, he got through each day thinking of the affection and conversations he received last weekend. Admittedly some of it came from donning the Monk's outfit, but he liked to think the friendly charming self inside was released at the market.

So up and down the aisles he went, hour by hour, day by day, fondly anticipating the arrival of next Saturday.

NEW ME

The more I play in different situations, the more I discover what I can do.

CHICK COREA

Most artists prefer subdued daylight to work by. Not Rachel Elliott. Her works rendered more intensely when bathed in brilliant sunlight. Colors were richer, textures stronger, shadows sharper. It made her feel better as well.

This was just such a day. The windows of her studio were large, typical for a building on a late 19th century small town main street, letting the golden morning sun flood the room. The space was located over an attorney's office in Dawsonville, VA. She had chosen this second floor corner apartment for her studio just because of its ample exposure to daylight.

The main drag of Dawsonville was nondescript and only three blocks long. Lined with the usual assortment of drug store, accountants, cafes, laundry, boutiques and branch banks at street level. Over these were layered one and two bedroom apartments occasionally interrupted by a lawyer's office or insurance firm. Rachel had purchased the end unit of the center block and remodeled it into her office-apartment-studio combination. Previously it was a dance studio, before that a Masonic Lodge.

The walls opposite the windows were covered with samples of previous artwork. Most were studies intended to fine tune the final product, but being of such fine quality, the uninitiated might have bought them as a premium artifact. It was an archive of the diverse media she excelled in -- painting, sculpture, lithography, jewelry.

Her father had been a facility specialist for the foreign service, coordinating renovations at embassies throughout Europe. To her, home was in a different country every few years. Her mother taught English and history, which enabled her to easily find work wherever dad was stationed. Both parents appreciated the arts, and took her and her younger brother to museums, plays and concerts in London, Paris, Rome, Austria and Copenhagen. A creative spark ignited in her early, which led to advanced studies in the cultural centers of Europe, refining a discipline and talent that put her works into respected galleries. It was hard to categorize her style since it was personal and ever changing but most curators pegged her as contemporary.

All of her professional development ultimately led to this project at these three butcher block tables lined up in the center. As if mesmerized by the adornments on the wall, 9 clay busts stared silently forward without blinking. They appeared identical, even when compared closely to its partner on either side. The figures on either end however were clearly two different people when brought together.

Rachel was totally immersed in the zone since she was within a few finishing touches of completing the last face. It was everything she envisioned it would be. Not striking, not beautiful, not familiar. Just plain, ordinary but a totally different look from the head she started out with at the other end of the table. The one that perfectly resembled her -- Rachel Elliot.

She was excited now, having reached this point after several months of intense trial and error. The idea congealed last fall, but started out as merely an incidental study occasionally fit in between work on other commissions. As she reflected on the creative possibilities and implications for her life, the lure became too much. Once her artwork was delivered, total focus turned to realizing this new vision. A few details remained to be selected-- hair style, eye color and other changes to work out, but everything was beginning to fall into place.

Just then her cell phone made a chirping sound. It was her automatic reminder for a lunch date with Dale. Time stood still whenever she was caught in the gravity of her work, so she depended heavily on the automatic reminders to keep appointments with clients, suppliers and friends. She gave the new face a kiss on the forehead, then ran into the apartment side for a quick shower.

The Manisa Cafe was conveniently located one block down the street. Like so many shops along main street, the space had reincarnated several times since originally opening its doors in the late 1800's as Smith's Tea and Pie Shoppe. The built-in kitchen layout helped guarantee that food establishments would occupy the space in the intervening decades. The embossed tin ceiling panels, dark old trim and brass fittings remained unchanged from opening day.

The latest owners migrated from Turkey and offered Mediterranean fare, thus drawing many from the artists' community. Another pull was that artists could display their works for sale which in turn enhanced the quality of the dining experience.

Behind the long narrow dining room was the kitchen. A corridor skirting around it led back to a compact but intimate eating area. It was intended for small group parties or private dining for special regulars. Most of Manisa's clientele were regulars anyway.

Rachel hurried through the front and made her way to their favorite table by the window where Dale was already seated.

Dale Marks was an electrician whom she met shortly after moving to Dawsonville. He wired her studio for the kilns and pottery wheels she used in her work, but it evolved into more of a relationship since on the side, he produced sculptures of his own. He made complex geometric assemblies from curved conduits interlaced with multicolored wires. The result possessed an industrial yet graceful quality which Rachel admired.

"So how was the gallery opening last night?" she asked while sliding into her chair "Bigger turnout than I expected, considering it was a Wednesday," he answered, "A few collectors even showed up from Charlotte and Philly. There were only 6 of us exhibiting but I think people were impressed with the high level of work here."

Katy, their waitress, appeared in an instant. "The usual?"

"Yes, I bet you know what it is," Dale replied.

"For the young lady, a vegetable plate with hummus. For you sir, a grilled pork sandwich with fennel and a side of lentil soup. Am I close?" Katy offered.

Dale did a thumbs up and said, "Tell the manager to keep you"

On the way to the kitchen she said, "He has to. I'm his niece."

Dale resumed his train of thought with Rachel, "It's too bad you couldn't make it last night. It was a great networking opportunity. I really thought you'd stop by."

"I considered it, but I was on a roll. Not a good time to stop," Rachel explained with some trepidation. She knew where this conversation was going.

"You mean on that morphing project you've been transfixed with. I don't want to sound intrusive but it sounds like it has taken over your life."

"You're almost right," she said calmly, without getting defensive. "I'm taking total control of my own life. And it may be in a way that no one has attempted before."

"How so? You're toying with the idea of changing your appearance. How is that any different from what they do in witness protection programs or celebrities going under the knife?"

"This isn't something I'm forced to do because my life is in danger. Trust me, I'm not a racketeer informant running from the Mafia. Totally voluntary, my own willing choice.

"And unlike movie stars or someone who is self-conscious about what they perceive as a flaw in their appearance, I personally have no misgivings about how I look now. There's nothing I need to fix.

"Or to make another comparison, I'm not looking to be another Frank Abagnale, conning money and favors out of others with multiple disguises."

Still probing but trying to show he was on her side, Dale led with a compliment, "I agree, you have looks that most young women would die for. Just doesn't seem worth tampering with."

"Thanks. I realize that up to now people have only seen a negative side: Fake or stolen personas to steal, or freakish outcomes from cosmetic surgery. But there is a fundamental underlying difference between those dark stories and my idea. In their case, despite the fact they were pretending to be someone else, or just wanted to improve their looks, they were essentially the same person inside. Ultimately they're the same me, I'm looking at the possibility of a new me."

Dale was quiet, at a loss for what to say next. He wasn't even clear how he felt about her ideas.

A moment of pause was provided when Katy returned with their food. Once she confirmed they had all they needed, she left to take orders from the lunch crowd that was beginning to fill the front side of the house.

Rachel and Dale had dated sporadically for several

years. Their vocations though were obstacles to fostering any measure of intimacy. Both kept erratic hours and frequently traveled. Her for shows and clients, him for building projects. There was a fondness they had for each other, but their relationship was at most one of best friends. Dale sensed the seriousness of the moment and felt he needed to share his concerns.

"You're already doing so well. I just don't see why you would even consider changing a thing. Did something happen while growing up?" he hesitated, then confessed, "I've never really come out and said this, but I care about you Rachel. I just don't know what it would be like if you weren't you anymore"

After few bites she said, "There is no emotional baggage I suffered from as a kid. My parents were great. They opened up the world to me. More importantly the world of art. From that, I realized it wasn't just the artworks themselves that excited me, it was the process of making something new --- the act of creating.

"Then a little over a year ago, I saw an exhibit at the Benson School of Art. There were photographs of students who had painted their faces in a variety of abstract designs. Their assignment had probably been to use their skin as a canvas. You could see an underlying goal of challenging the viewer to accept individualized diversity in the extreme.

"That isn't what I saw though. Then and there, I saw the possibility of creating a new self. This is my passion, creating. But what greater challenge could there be than creating yourself.

"Think about it, most of our identity is set in our

teen years, and most of that given to us by others. Parents, family, teachers, friends, bosses and many others in some way shape who we are. Sure, as young adults we start making decisions on our own, but that is layered over values and habits already fixed beforehand. The exciting thing is that once arriving at that point, our society now has enough tools at our disposal that we can take charge and re-make ourselves- create a new identity."

Dale nibbled and poked at his food in silence, unable to digest his lunch or her comments very well. Finally, he said, "I'm happy here. I could always learn more for my job or craft, but otherwise can't see a rhyme or reason for changing my personality. Yes, I travel a lot for work, but it's a comfort to have a home base with family and friends to come back to."

"And you should hold on to that. You grew up here. Your people would be concerned if they saw any major changes in your life. What's the matter with Dale they would be thinking. He's not acting like himself. I don't have that. My parents are gone and my brother is busy with his family, so we rarely talk. I'm totally free to exercise creativity on myself.

"And more than that, I envision having fresh experiences, seeing everyday events from an entirely different perspective as a new person, not from the context of who I used to be."

Rachel was on another plane from Dale, so there was not much he could offer. "I just don't think it's a good idea, but I know you have a mind of your own. Just be careful and don't jump into something you might regret later." Changing the subject he said, "Before I forget, you remember that out of town job I told you about last month?"

"Yes, some bank office building in Charlotte. Next month as I remember."

"That's it. Well my boss called me late last night. Said they needed me to go down earlier, like next week to help straighten out the mess. Seems they're way behind schedule. I may have to work there several months instead of a few weeks. I don't mind the extra money though."

"Good deal. Don't let them overwork you. Accidents can happen when you're tired."

They finished lunch soon after that.

Rachel nearly broke out into a sprint on her way back to the studio, even though it was only a few blocks away. The whole discussion made her eager to dive back into her work. Neither had finished their meal, so they ended it with a long hug and Dale picked up the check.

It was obvious he just wasn't getting it at all, causing her to stop short of telling him everything, mainly that she had already decided to move ahead. She was excited about the future, yet she felt a seed of melancholy realizing this was probably the last time they would see each other.

She had to chuckle at the image looking in the mirror. Small multicolored strips covered her face. What to call them: Rainbow measles, Kandinsky face, paintball loser?

In a corner of the studio a makeshift boudoir had been set up. Sitting on a cosmetic stand beside it was a tube of 'primer', a tray of strips called Epidermilite, a spray 'fixer' and a jar of medicated cream to treat any rash or irritation resulting from the procedure.

This four step process was called Visagin and named after a town in Latvia where the key ingredient was discovered and mined. It was not a treatment that had to be continually refreshed, but effected permanent alterations. What Rachel liked about it were the multiple sets of patches, engineered to either expand or shrink to varying degrees the underlying structures of the skin, all with nearly pinpoint accuracy.

Visagin was developed in response to the ever growing demand by the public for tools of beauty. The drive persisted around the world for centuries but in recent decades it intensified, causing proliferation of numerous approaches including shots, pills, diets, creams and ultraviolet light. Where once going under the knife was reserved for movie stars and patients with deformities, it was now commonplace. It was only a matter of time before an over-the-counter product like Visagin hit the market that approximated the results of cosmetic surgery. England, Brazil and eastern European countries had given their approval, but it was stalled in a jurisdictional dispute between the FDA and the surgeon general's office. Fortunately, Rachel was able to easily purchase a kit over the internet.

Rachel meticulously continued to apply more patches to her face using bust Number 8 as a guide. The clay models she had just finished were not intended as individual studies, but were the sequence to be followed, a kind of three-dimensional set of instructions.

As a youngster, Rachel had taken sketching classes at the London Portraiture Gallery. One lesson that stayed with her was the fact that when it came to faces, subtle changes had major impacts. Over 7 billion people on this planet share the same features: eyes, eyebrows, nose, mouth, cheeks and ears -- arranged together in a common structure. And yet within these strict boundaries, little differences produced endless variety.

Rachel understood this. It was the core of her strategy. She wasn't after a radically glamorous makeover. By all accounts she was average. Average height, weight and looks. Her transformation would still be to a normal, perhaps plain woman -- just different. As simple as it sounded, it was a monumental test of her artistic skills. And she loved it.

The area between the eyes and chin required the most work. It was a complex combination of convex and concave surfaces, but Visagin let her use her sculpting skills. A warm tingling sensation could be sensed but nothing severe. If this was the worst it got, the next six steps would be a breeze. It would take a couple weeks to complete which was to be expected.

While the patches were at work, her attention turned to eyebrows. A little thinner and slight change in arch. Plucking was something she'd have to make a routine from now on but pencil liner was out of the question. She wasn't fixated on how things looked at the moment. This was going to be a process.

Rachel would let her hair grow out in the next few weeks. She had always worn it short just for the ease of personal maintenance and perhaps from her mother's example. By letting it go to shoulder length and keeping it straight, it narrowed the shape of her face without adding too much grooming time. For that same reason she elected not to color it. That could change if she were so inclined down the road.

Two hours later the patches came off and the fixer applied. Several minutes passed then that was washed off and the medicated cream applied. Dusk was settling in and the apartment growing dark, so Rachel switched on some lights, and went into the kitchenette where she poured a glass of merlot.

Just inside the entrance from the stair was a casual sitting area. It served double duty as a client meeting space and her living room. There she planted herself on the big cushy sofa, and watched the sky fade into night. She was exhausted from the focused tasks, yet still keyed up from the fact she was well on her way toward her goal. It would take a while to really relax.

"Next is Case File - General Claims CC322- Petition to Change Name. Will the applicant please come forward," directed the County Clerk.

Rachel approached the podium in front of Judge Jacob Halward in the 16th General Circuit Court in Culpeper, Virginia. Friday mornings were reserved for uncontested civil cases and two others had just finished ahead of her. The judge looked over the paperwork for a minute then said,

"Please state your name"

"Rachel Elliott, your honor"

"And you wish to change your name?"

"That's correct, sir."

"There are certain conditions required by statute that I will ask you to attest to."

"I understand."

"Is this for the purpose of avoiding debt obligations?"

"No it is not. I included a credit report and a bank statement with my application to confirm my financial condition."

The judge looked up and smiled. "Thank you Ms. Elliott but it was not necessary. Your notarized signature was sufficient. Is this change for fraudulent purposes or intended to deceive others?"

"No, sir."

"And you're not acquiring the name as a result of marriage."

"No I'm not. I am single."

"And you wish to go by the name of Manita Bovaris"

"I do."

He gave it a minute to sink in, then said, "It doesn't appear to be a frivolous name, or a rip off of some publicly well-known celebrity."

"I hope not. I spent a good deal of time creating and researching it."

Judge Halward looked intently at the application again and looked perplexed.

"Just why do you wish to change your name? I don't see anything onerous with the name Rachel Elliott. On the form, under reason, you just wrote the word 'choice'."

"Yes, I agree, it's an ok name. However, when I was born, I had no name. My parents selected a name. The state did not select it, nor evaluate it. They merely accepted it as part of the recording of my birth without my input. Now that I am of capacity, I wish to exercise my free will and make my own choices of who I am and what I do, including my identity of which my name is a large part. So in a way I am re-registering the name, submitted by the person who it is attached to - who in effect owns it. I am requesting the change as common law under the 'usage' principle."

That last part she learned while reading up on the subject at the library. It had its effect. The judge was silent for a moment while he pondered the subject. Thinking out loud he said, "State law is specific about what constitutes a name change that is unacceptable, which doesn't apply here. Where it is not definitive is what constitutes an acceptable change. In practice, typical renaming has occurred for marriages and divorces."

"If I may submit, Your Honor, from my limited reading there is great latitude on the part of government agencies in granting changes. Federal agencies liberally allow immigrants to revise their names to ones sounding more 'Americanized'. And again, all parents are given a free pass to submit any name they wish to vital statistics."

Judge Halward laid her folder down, sat more upright and said, "Insofar as the state has afforded me broad discretionary authority in this matter, I find there would be no harm to the community with this change. I confess I don't fully understand your motivation, but I do comprehend how this is highly personal. Since common law does lean toward the individual, I will rule in your favor. Petition granted."

"Thank you very much, your honor," Manita said simply, turning to leave.

"One last question."

"Yes, sir?" she asked, a little nervous at the unexpected interruption.

He squinted at something on one of the pages, looked up at her, then commented, "You look very different than this picture on your driver's license."

Internally she tensed, hoping it didn't show on the surface. The subject of her metamorphosis was not something to cover in this forum. She returned, "The photo id is three years old. I swear the cameras are programmed to humble you. I've been working out since then. Hopefully, I show some improvement."

Noticing the court had filled in with more claimants, he returned to the docket. "All to the good. You have a good day Ms. Bovaris. Clerk, next case please."

Rachael, now Manita, hurried to her car in the parking garage next door. She wasted no time in getting to Route 234 and headed east toward Fredericksburg. Her heart was still racing, but not so much from the courtroom experience itself. She had been confident the application would be approved. A lawyer friend had confided with her that Judge Halward would be the most open minded of the options at that court. What was exciting was hearing the Judge say Manita. That was the first time someone addressed her by her new name. Since her facial transition was still in progress, it was the hearing of the word that thrust her into her new being. Ready or not, Manita was born.

Manita had not told Dale everything. She was going to make her creation of self as all-encompassing as possible. That meant changing more than her face. With her renaming now official, the next stop was her optician's office. She had an appointment to get a set of new contact lenses. She had glasses, but only needed them for close-up work, such as crafting intricate jewelry. By switching to contacts she was able to add color. The dark brown she selected gave more punch to her eyes than her current hazel shade.

Other stops included the post office, Social Security and MetroTrust bank. The DMV would wait until she completed the Visagin phases. The id photo had to show her final state.

After changing her accounts and applying for a new charge card at the bank, she went shopping for a new wardrobe at Liberty Mall. Her artistic background tended to make her fussy about visual details, which added a lot of time to her decision making. In a desire to drop some tendencies of the old Rachael, she decided to defer to the services of a personal shopper.

Upon arrival at a small parlor on the third floor at Thompkins Department Store, a young, tall, smartly dressed woman approached and introduced herself, "Good afternoon, welcome to Thompkins. Are you Ms. Manita Bovaris?"

"Yes I am," Manita replied.

"Wonderful. I'm Becky Gravella, your Fashion Consultant. Please follow me back to our Design Center."

Becky led Manita down a softly lit corridor to a hexagon shaped salon with plush red carpet and indirect lighting. Most of the walls were clad in full length mirrors except where interrupted by doors leading to dressing rooms. Furniture consisted of a glass table serving as a desk, two cushioned chairs, and another table with coffee, tea and a water flask.

"Please have a seat," Becky said as she motioned to a chair. "Can I get you something to drink?"

"No thank you."

"Now then, what would we like to accomplish this afternoon? You said over the phone that you were looking to make a change."

Rachel had never dressed the part of an artist. She could not embrace the stereotypes of the profession. No hippie smocks and layers of beads, no Gothic garb or peasant dresses, no berets, denim jackets, pointy cowboy boots, or Carol Channing glasses. The focus was never about herself. People remembered her for her artwork, not for some subculture manner of dress. American casual comfort was her style of choice. Usually jeans and a plain blouse. The biggest decision each day was whether to wear tennis shoes or flip-flops.

"That's right. I've tended to be rather informal in my apparel. I work independently without much need to dress up for anyone. Now I'm at a point where I want to step up another level."

"Is this for work or an upcoming event?"

"No, just personal reasons. Something I need to do. I want to keep it simple and practical. Good quality but not showy. Refined but not racy. I'm throwing out a lot of ideas that sound senseless."

"Oh, no. Quite the contrary. I fully understand. We definitely have exactly what you want. Why don't we just go ahead and get started."

Two hours into the session, they took a short break. In that time, one pair of slacks, one skirt, and two shirts had been selected. Manita had avoided directing Becky on what to try, but she did approach it in a way she hated in other situations. She didn't know exactly what she wanted, but she would know it when she saw it.

"Have you given any thought to accessories or jewelry?" Becky asked.

"I do have this one item that's special to me. I'll probably wear it frequently," Manita answered while reaching into her purse. She pulled out a necklace and showed it to Becky. In a two-inch oval of polished silver was a collection of tiny colored glass pieces assembled to resemble a miniature stained glass window. Inlaid in the design were script letters spelling out Manita.

"Wow, that is exquisite." Becky exclaimed. "Who made that for you?"

"Oh, somebody I used to know. This is one of her last pieces. Eventually other pieces would be good, but I'll pick them out later." As Rachel, she had no attraction to earrings and bracelets, however they did have a way of drawing the eye and changing the way one perceived another's face. This could help her new look.

After more hours and outfits, Manita was back on the road to Dawsonville. Becky had graciously stayed after the store closed to ensure Manita was fully accommodated. The result was a trunk full of new clothes.

WeeSee was an upstart news company with offices in a new building on Milwaukee Street in Wicker Park, an increasingly gentrified neighborhood in northwest Chicago. WeeSee was one of the Chicago

Tribunes' several forays into Internet publishing. Its concept was to select and train small volunteer teams of writers and photographers, typically blogger types, in each neighborhood of which the city had many. Each group would cover stories they would sniff out in their respective areas, in addition to others assigned by central staff. A fee would be paid for each story submitted. In a way, it was crowdsourcing the news. Each day it was distributed online with limited print circulation.

Manita and Rav Panyel were partners on one of several permanent teams in the home office. He had a degree in English and a masters in communications, so he handled the writing. She was their photographer. As universally understood, most good jobs are filled through connections. Manita landed this one through a friend of her father's. Mather Stiles was an executive for a chain of radio stations and knew the industry well, companies large and small. She had confided in him her plans. Looking upon her as a second niece, he paved the way for the job change. Going this route avoided the complications of a formal application. Between samples of photography from university courses, and selected pieces of graphic materials, she was able to assemble an impressive portfolio that demonstrated her ample capabilities.

Friday morning, the six teams assembled for their standard recap and planning session. This was where story possibilities were reviewed and assigned for the next week. Bianca Kelly, the editor of WeeSee, led the group through its paces, first starting out by having each team recount any challenges or observations about their stories. Next she summarized a report covering feedback and hits to the website which were growing each week.

"Manita and Rav, your article on the changing mix of populations in the neighborhood must have struck a nerve. It received many comments and most of them favorable."

"Nice to hear." Rav acknowledged, "We learned a lot about the community from doing that. It gave us some ideas for follow up"

"The photos that went with it were outstanding, Manita. They put the readers right into the place. And the people too. One felt like they knew them, without a word being said. You seem to have a special knack for capturing faces."

"Thanks," she said simply, without encouraging further dialogue on that subject.

"We might have something here. I would like you two to put together something down on the South Side. I know it's outside your territory, but for now consider the boundaries soft."

Rav, who grew up in Chicago, quickly asked, "There are some rough parts over there. What angle do you have in mind?"

"You only hear about the area in the regular news outlets when there is trouble. I think there is a human interest side yet to be told, especially on the impact with kids. Just a hunch, I believe in going where our competitors haven't."

"We can drive there this afternoon," Manita offered, "and scope out the possibilities."

"Up to you."

"I'm game," Rav responded.

On the drive down I94, Manita and Rav strategized on how to organize their afternoon. They were heading toward Myers Community Center. They had called ahead for permission from the center director. It was an ideal location to find a good many young people in one place after school. To start out, they would split up. He would take a sampling of interviews; she would photograph the general setting to establish context. On the way back, they would plan the detail work for the week that followed.

It was a three block drive west off the freeway. The building was a plain yellow brick 1950's era middle school that was converted to a rec center after the last round of school closures. They parked, then climbed the steps at the main entrance, passing three teenagers hanging out beside the door. After checking in at the front desk, they proceeded down long corridors. How little schools had changed over the years. Today schools were a little brighter and colorful, but painted concrete block was still the material of choice.

They passed rooms with different activities already in progress. Ping pong, foos ball and air hockey were active in one wing. In another, younger boys and girls were being tutored in remedial math. In the rooms with those learning English, sentences rolled out in foreign languages -- maybe Spanish and African, but it was hard to make out the dialect for sure. It was one of these rooms that Rav staked his claim. Manita went on to the big room at the end of the hall.

A quality of many older schools were the cavernous spaces they contained. The gym Manita walked into was spacious -- big enough for two basketball courts. High schoolers had commandeered both while a younger group, likely ten to fourteen year olds, sat in the bleachers impatiently waiting their turn. She unpacked her camera, began clicking away, and scouted the floor for unique shots. As she positioned herself around the room, the teams generally ignored her in favor of trying for three pointers. If they had been in a refereed game, most would have fouled out.

Leaning back against the wall opposite the stands, she zoomed and panned, studiously picking out views from the camera display she used as a viewfinder. Her stare locked onto a boy sitting by himself high up in the stands. He appeared to be watching her every move, ignoring the two games underway. Completing her circle around the courts, she climbed the risers and sat down next to the boy. His faded jeans and striped tee-shirt were ill-fitting for his slight frame. She could tell he was nervous and shy from his restless leg syndrome and slight retreat from her approach.

"Hi, my name is Manita. What's yours?"

"Damion," he replied, barely audible.

"Do you go to school near here?"

"Yes, ma'am. Raymond Elementary."

Even though he was reserved, she could see a stirring of curiosity in his eyes, especially for the camera.

"I'm here with another person to do a story about the neighborhood. Tell me, Damion, what do like about living here?"

"We just moved here from Detroit so grandma could get some work. I don't know much about the place."

Getting off that track Manita changed the subject. "My job is to take pictures. Would you like to see what I have so far?"

He nodded eagerly. While they looked together at the shots on the little screen, she occasionally glanced at him. It may have been an overabundance of imagination, but she detected an avid excitement akin to her own drive for artistic discovery.

"You take good pictures, ma'am. What's your name, again?"

"Thank you. It's Manita."

"Miss Manita, could you teach me how to do that?"

"Sure. I could make up some lessons for you. You'd have to check with your mom and dad first."

"I don't live with mom and dad. I live with my grandma and 3 sisters. My sisters are in art class right now."

"Tell you what. I'll write a note to your grandma with my name and number. She can call me if it's ok with her. Sound good?"

"Yes, good," he said, smiling.

She pulled out a business card from her case, wrote a note on the back and handed it to Damion. On an impulse, she handed the camera over to him.

"Go ahead. Take one look through the little window, then press the big round button on top. Take your time. Wait for one that looks really good."

It was a big, bulky professional unit, so he had to hold it with both hands while she helped steady it. After a few moments he took his shot.

She looked it over closely. He had caught one of the teens slam dunking the ball.

"That's really pretty good." she remarked, "I think we could have some fun with this."

Finally, Manita got up to leave. "I have to get back to work right now. Hope your grandma can call. Nice meeting you, Damion."

He held his hand up in a timid wave.

As the sun set on that day, Manita turned on some soft music before stepping out onto her small postage stamp balcony. With a cup of hot chocolate, she sat down and looked out over the panorama of lights in the distance. Her apartment on the seventh floor in Naperville faced south with a clear view of the towers that populated downtown. The only recognizable shapes were the Willis and Hancock buildings. It was Friday evening and time to decompress and reflect on how far she had come.

Despite the many changes accomplished in a relatively short period, she surprised even herself at how smoothly it went, and at how seemingly effortless it was to detach herself from the person who was Rachel. She supposed it was something like reincarnation, except instead of transforming into another lifeform in another lifetime, she created another being within the same lifespan. Reincarnation wasn't the best word. Maybe replace or supplant was better. A vessel had been emptied and was refilling with a new formulation.

Up until now, most of the changes within her were selected by her. Going forward her new environment and experiences would have their own effect upon her. Little differences were already creeping into her daily routine. She used to be a morning person. Now job schedules pressed upon her to work extra hours and keep awake later into the evening. Dawsonville had no happy hour. Here the guys went out every third night, leading her to socialize to a greater extent. It proved to be the best way to keep up with internal politics.

And then there was Damion. His grandmother had called and they worked out a plan for some lessons. She had never felt much in the way of maternal instincts, yet the young boy appeared to have some potential she could foster. She was sure to continue to evolve but that was exciting in itself. She knew who she was now. Who would she be a year or two down the road?

And beyond that? The potential was there to do this again. And again. A person could live many lives in a lifetime. But that would come later. It was good to be Manita and she would stay focused on that.

That same evening, Dale pulled up the gravel drive to his house. The few lights that were on from a timer gave the place a welcoming glow. He had just driven non-stop from Charlotte, made the more grueling by unusually heavy weekend traffic. Right now, a hot shower and a cold beer were his only obsessions. He flipped on more lights and threw his jacket and keys on the sofa. His suitcase and cooler he would retrieve from the truck later. Heading for the shower, he noticed a square cube box wrapped in colorful paper sitting on the coffee table. He opened it up and there it was -- the clay bust of a familiar face. Smiling, he lifted it out carefully and placed it on the table. In the bottom was a folded note. It read:

"Rachel Elliot stopped here."

HOLD THAT THOUGHT

When you're successful, things have a momentum and you can't tell If you have created the momentum or it's creating you.

DAVE LIEBMAN

"My name is Peter Catoya. I am a research scientist and work for Mindco in Basehore, Kansas. My family and I live in Fairmont, another suburb of Kansas City, Kansas.

I begin this recording with some regret for not having started it sooner. Scientists long ago, like Albert Einstein, Thomas Edison and Galileo, used to keep handwritten journals. If I did that, I would probably fall into my habit of writing only about things of a technical nature. I prefer this cell phone which makes it easier for me to freely collect thoughts that are more personal.

Looking back, it's no surprise how I came to be

doing what I do today. As a kid, I was always fascinated with how things worked. Maybe I got that from my dad who was always fixing up old sports cars. But not being mechanically inclined myself, I developed an interest in anatomy around the time I took biology in high school. Our school system was pretty advanced, so computers were mainstream in the classroom and I picked up some programming skills in the technology club after school. I discovered in college that the newly emerging field of bio-engineering contained all my areas of interest, so that's what I majored in.

College is also where I met my love, Kelly. We were matched by our close circle of friends who we continue to see today. Kelly is the balancing force in my life, trying valiantly but not always preventing me from floating off into the nether world of science. Up to recently, she had to continually remind me of ordinary things I had to do at home.

After graduation, I was fortunate enough to land a series of assignments and promotions that solidified my career within the field. Now my work history sounds boring when I recite it back to myself. Lab Assistant at K-Tech, assistant professor in biology and research team lead at Wichita State, bio-engineering chair at the Jansen Institute. But I can see how events at work and home conspired to bring me to Mindco.

Titles sound nice, but once you get a family, it's time to make money. When our son Hunter -- by the way, John Hunter was an anatomy expert in London.

I couldn't resist -- was born, we moved back to Fairmont. There I went into the private sector and got a job at Bold Way Pharmaceuticals, not too far away in Bonner Springs. Next came Maria, our daughter -- thank Maria Lick, a physiologist, for her name. Kelly protested my name choices at first, but eventually they grew on her.

I was especially drawn to Bold Way by their unique business model. They weren't trying to become some huge mega corp, at least not in the beginning. They were looking to establish a specialized niche, kind of like a technology startup, but for medicine. Martin Laars, the CEO and founder, is in fact a techy himself. Came from San Jose and saw how ideas came to life. Maybe that's where he got the idea for this. His vision is to offer solutions that are not strictly medicine nor equipment nor diet nor surgery. Maybe the answer for some ailments is a combination or blend of several approaches. This means bridging some disciplines that in academia will never fly. It is a way of working I find exciting and can relate to.

At this point, I had everything I wanted. So I thought. A well-paying job doing what I liked. Even some potential to get to the top as the company grew. A great family living in a nice community with good schools. Kelly was and is the organizer at home even though she works in communications at an insurance company. Thank heavens. Not that I am disorganized, but sometimes I can get so excited and focused when I'm deep in an experiment that I lose awareness of important things around me.

And then the big opportunity came. I remember the day well when Martin called me into his office to chat. He noted how for many years, studies of the brain had been under way at several universities. It was an expanding field of inquiry - one of the hot new frontiers of investigation. Martin wanted to capitalize on this, and his assessment was that we were better positioned than anyone else to develop advances, get them patented and quickly bring them to market.

So he floated the idea of setting up a special unit. He saw enormous potential to not only tackle existing brain ailments and damage, but to find ways to enhance thinking in otherwise normal people. We could move from fixing the body to making it better. Martin's voice crescendoed into overtones of enthusiasm that were so contagious, my own mind began racing through the possibilities.

After pouring out all the ideas that he had been building up for some time, Martin asked me pleadingly to head up a team of top notch scientists to invent new products and processes targeting brain function. I didn't need convincing.

He literally gave me carte-blanche to mobilize the operation. I could hire, equip and house however I thought best. The only requirements from Martin were to keep this strictly confidential, the work take place at a remote site, reach way outside the box, and keep him informed.

I couldn't contain my excitement when I got

home. The minute I walked in the door, I repeated the whole conversation, word for word, to Kelly. She was happy for me and could see the upward trajectory for our family. Her only concern was how much this new venture would consume me and the impact on our personal life. I promised then to keep things in balance but eventually she turned out to be right.

My first order of business was to set up a lab. I found the perfect spot in a light industrial area on the edge of Basehore. It had been a manufacturing company that mass produced small electrical motors but folded long ago. The structure had an abundance of electrical capacity which was what we needed. Scanners, lasers, 3D printers and two MRI machines suck up a lot of power. The plain concrete block building had sat empty for quite a while but a fresh coat of paint inside and out was all it needed. No new walls to start with. A wide open lab gave us the flexibility to change directions easily. Once a security fence was installed clear round with controlled access, we had a bona fide skunkworks.

The location continues to be great because of its convenience to home, headquarters and the big city in case unique resources are needed. It particularly came in handy when we progressed to the level of testing on animals. It took a while to be certified, so this work had to be done back at the Bonner facility.

Hiring top notch scientists fell into place too. I had a broad network of contacts from my previous jobs and they were all too eager to jump ship. The salaries, benefits, hours and cutting edge innovation I offered made leaving their dreary political bureaucracies a no brainer. I tapped Ty Borwensky, from K-Tech, as my lab manager. He knew the government regs and industry best practices inside and out and I personally had seen how well he could run research programs. As time went on, Ty became my right hand man, second in command and confidante.

The reason I created Ty's position was because of how I planned to attack our mission. Generally, I approach challenges like this with a gunshot method. If I don't have a clear picture in mind of where I want to end up, I try different directions at the same time. Here this meant having maybe 6 teams, each with their own set of experiments, testing different hypothesis proposed either by other investigators or implied by previous studies.

Despite all the prestigious schools studying the mind, the knowledge base was and is very weak. The whole enterprise of mind mapping that everyone's so excited about has serious deficiencies. For instance, the models depicting various centers such as a motor control center, the sensing center and an emotional center are way over simplified. Looking at the real brain, there are no centers. It's more like an inscrutable tangle of wires which happen to be extremely small. There is more interaction throughout this arrangement than we can understand today.

The other problem with mind mapping is that it doesn't really explain how and why the brain functions the way it does. Lots of theories abound but no real evidence. Compare it to a car's engine. You can look under the hood and locate the battery, steering column, engine block, radiator and other parts. But just looking at them and knowing where they are doesn't tell you how they work together and in the end what makes the car go.

At the start of our work, I studied the literature on these subjects anyway, just to see what solid scientific tidbits I could build on. I also checked back on my biology and physiology roots for inspiration.

It's clear to me now that right around this time Kelly noticed things that told her I was slipping into old habits. There were little things like forgetting to stop by the grocery store for some ingredient needed for dinner that night. Or driving past the turn to her parents' house on a weekend visit, even though we'd been there hundreds of times and I should have gotten there on auto-pilot.

These were lapses most people experienced but I certainly understood how they annoyed Kelly. Given my passion for the project and intense, and admittedly narrow focus, I directed at finding promising paths forward, I brushed aside the issue as something checklists and reminders could easily fix. There are so many apps and programs for that these days.

Throughout the next year, our Mindco teams settled into each of their exploratory tracks. I'll simplify this part and avoid a lot details since the technical data will be in our scientific articles to be written later. Most of it is proprietary anyway.

The first group took a fresh look at how mind

mapping is performed. The huge metal cocoons called MRIs in use seemed prehistoric to us. They are expensive, inefficient, static and for my mind lacked the detail to match the billions of neurons that held so many secrets. It's like looking at an atom through a telescope. Our machine needed to read microscopically and dynamically. A video was going to tell us more than a snapshot.

It is understandable that researchers would prefer a visual model, which by its nature is over-simplified. The fact that brain activity is three dimensional in nature only compounds the problem. Our team decided only a powerful computer had the capacity to read a brain. To do this a 3-D addressing system was devised to map infinitesimally small data points throughout the gray matter. The group also created an ingenious way to scan, a method inspired by the electrical power companies.

Whenever there are short circuits or outages on the power grid, the utility is able to quickly pinpoint their location based on the dynamics of electrical current. We used the same principle on the body. By using the spinal cortex as one of the electrode connections and two additional on either side of the head, we had the necessary triangulation to cover a solid mass.

A different team tackled the issue of intervention. Other parts of the human body such as arms and legs are more readily accessible for physical procedures. Getting at and manipulating the brain is another matter altogether. We were scientists, not doctors, so surgery was out of the question.

Success again. The group determined that the same pathways that brought signals out during monitoring could be used as a guidance system to direct whatever substance or product we devised to a preselected target area. Eyes, ears, nose and other body parts have neural connections that eventually carry electrical/chemical signals back to the brain. This in concert with other procedures proved surprisingly effective.

The other study groups labored over techniques hoping to bolster the mental machine. This proved a tougher nut to crack with too many questions unanswered. Did thought reside in the cell cores or in the neurons themselves? Were certain mental states confined to regions of the brain as some have theorized, or is this a result of interplay across regions? Too much uncertainty! I became resigned to the fact we would have to use a trial and error approach. We would be happy to uncover anything that was successful, even if we didn't understand why it worked.

So we tried everything: enzymes, medicines, minerals, nutrients, radiation, all kinds of radio waves, and a few stem cells. Thinking outside the box, even some low grade viruses were tested. This took up a lot of time and led us down many dead ends. Of course no human subjects were involved at this stage. All the experiments were performed on mice and monkeys. We did have access to human brain tissue from the county coroner's office which helped.

Around mid-June of last year, Mindco reached its first year of operation. It seemed like a good time for Kelly and I to take our family on a much needed vacation. We didn't go too far. We rented a cabin at Penguin Corners for a week. Penguin Corners is a campground catering to children not far from El Dorado State Park. Several days were spent at poolside watching Hunter and Maria romping in the kiddy pool. It's funny. Today I can vividly remember watching them climbing on a simulated iceberg in the Antarctica playground. I can even picture the giant concrete penguins that guarded the iceberg but at the time I was too engrossed in my own thoughts to make note of anything in that moment.

We did make it over to the park for a walk around the lake which for me was the most peaceful. Otherwise, I can't say I felt unfettered joy on the trip as a whole. It was more of a respite for Kelly than for me. Not that I don't love Kelly and the kids, but my thoughts were constantly overrun by obstacles on the projects that needed to be resolved. I kept thinking of tests to run when I got back. Every chance I got, I snuck a look at emails and progress reports from the team. It took a lot of will power to resist calling back with suggestions for the group.

When we returned I was pleased to discover the teams had done just fine without me. In fact, the group looking at neuron enhancement came across a few proteins that looked promising. Mice injected with them appeared more alert and learned remarkably faster in the exercises they were given.

During the weeks that followed, two other events forced me to reorient my thinking. On Saturdays mornings, I typically take the kids to an arts and crafts workshop for preschoolers at our local community center while Kelly stays at home doing the laundry. On this particular morning, while they were creating masterpieces in their class, I walked over to the strip center across the street, got a cup of coffee then browsed through the bookshop next store. I realized I hadn't read a novel in quite a while, so I chatted with the clerk and got a list of titles of books I might like to read later.

One of the psychology books I scanned had a controversial theory on how people made decisions that I continued to mull that over when I returned to the car and headed back to the house. Turning the corner onto my block I got a call. It was Kelly asking where were I and the kids.

Inexplicably, I had forgotten and left them at the community center.

Needless to say, Kelly was extremely upset. I was embarrassed at myself and even surprised that I could do such a thing.

On the following Friday, Ty and I were working late pouring over progress reports, analyzing results and mapping out studies for the coming week. Around eight pm he came up to me and said he had to leave. He and his brood were leaving for a weekend family reunion in Kansas City. There was a brain scan still running on three mice, and would I mind completing it and shutting down the equipment when I left. Saying yes, I told him to leave and have a good time. Kelly had taken the kids over to visit their grandparents for the evening, so there was no rush for me to get home. He left and as I continued to piece together the data, I became more comfortable that our efforts were bearing fruit and by the end of the year we could produce some effective treatments.

The following Monday I came in early to ready the shop for the day's work. I unlocked the door and the moment I stepped in, I heard multiple beeping alarms. Running to the back, I knew immediately what it was. I had forgotten to close down the equipment the previous Friday. Three mice lay dead in their glass experimental boxes with wires attached to their bodies. Lights were flashing on the adjacent monitors.

I quickly shut down the equipment then disposed of the animals per protocol. All this I did in a jumbled state of disbelief and anger at myself for doing such a stupid thing. Once the situation was stabilized, I made an urgent called for Ty to hurry into the office. Hopefully he could make it in ahead of the others.

We sat cloistered in my office for a couple of hours assessing any potential damage to the studies or the equipment. There didn't appear to be any permanent impacts we couldn't recover from, but obviously this couldn't happen again. It didn't make sense to create a new policy for the group when it was my failure to correct. We decided not to make any changes, but I definitely needed to be doing something different.

Ty was my friend that I could trust with personal issues, so I opened up about my frustration, and frankly some anxiety, over this event and the recent incident with the kids. Was this typical of people juggling loaded complex lives or was it something deeper? He confided that he in fact had seen other cases of my not recalling something important we had discussed but he had to remind me of. He too dismissed it to information overload or too many responsibilities. He didn't go so far as to call it a personal defect.

As we went further into the subject of memory, I realized we were in the perfect place to check it out. We had the equipment and the knowhow. I could see Ty did not share the wisdom of my idea. He was quick to say it was bad practice try out procedures oneself. And besides, we weren't approved for human trials yet.

But I persisted. I wasn't considering anything invasive or medicinal. Just some routine scans to see if any abnormalities showed up. I also knew Ty to be an impeccably careful scientist. Based on recent events, maybe more careful than myself.

That same day we developed a plan to quietly take multiple scans of my brain, preferably at different times of day for a month. Kelly could never find out. She would fiercely object which I could understand. I developed the ruse of taking the kids into the shop on weekends and evenings to see what daddy did at work. Kelly was happy to have them off her hands for a few hours here and there. I set up a controlled play area behind the building, then Ty put me through the routine.

It was odd at first to be on the receiving end of the experiment. The device I wore on my head was half helmet and half skull cap. Nicknamed the Commcap, it was 1/2 inch thick and stiff but flexible. It far exceeded traditional electrical encephalographs in the number of contact monitoring points it contained since each was a millimeter in size. In a way it was like a digital TV with millions of pixels that distribute a signal from a single source. This worked in reverse. Millions of micro sensors detected impulses and sent its type and amplitude back to the computer.

I had braced myself for some type of foreign sensation, but none came. There was a slight touch of coolness. My suspicion was this was the result of energy from my scalp absorbing into the cap. To concentrate on short term memory function, I looked at a series of words and pictures, each time stopping a moment in between to commit to memory. The computer captured the internal responses a millisecond after each viewing, assuming the mind was sending the perception off to the memory box at that very moment. In all, the procedure lasted twenty minutes.

Ty and I finished the scans weeks later. It was a tedious process to pour over the mountain of numbers. There were too many to humanly cover, so we had the computer summarize in the specific clusters that were suspect. My results were then compared against readings from normal subjects found in other studies. My fears were confirmed. The short term memory function of my brain was woefully weak.

Halfway through the study, I had already assumed the worst and began plotting my next steps. Now I had to implement them. This was a tough period. I had to pretend to Kelly, the kids, Laars and the staff that everything was ok and business as usual. Inwardly I was extremely anxious since I was embarking on a untried path that was potentially damaging or worse -- fatal.

This time I had to go it alone. Ty was not going to help perform these procedures on me. He couldn't, legally or ethically. Even though he believed in our goals, it was too soon to apply any of our treatments despite our early successes. He tried fervently to talk me out of it.

I on the other hand presented a confident front. I argued that none of the techniques were invasive. I suffered no ill effects from the cap, there were no reports in the literature that the chemicals I would receive were toxic, and I could terminate the procedure at any time.

Ty reluctantly conceded to be on standby in another part of shop should anything go awry. A panic buzzer was added to the setup so I could summon his help. On a cool sunny Saturday morning in October, with all the paraphernalia and precautions in place, I began the operation.

First I put on the Commcap. It would serve a different function this time. Instead of a diagnostic tool, it was used to detect any improvements in the firing of the neurons. Other nodes did the reverse. They sent mild pulses of energy to the very areas that were firing.

Then I took off my shoes and socks, and pasted one electrode each on my feet, followed by one on my lower back, then one on each middle finger. On a table beside me was a syringe and two bottles. One was a cocktail mix of proteins, the other a special formulation of minerals. I carefully mixed equal parts of each.

I pushed 'enter' to start the computer. After a minute, I took a deep breath, filled the syringe with our magic brew, then injected its contents into my right forearm. The next fifteen minutes were occupied by the same word and numbers game I played during the previous month's exercise.

The concept behind this set of tasks was fairly simple and quite exquisite as far as I was concerned. The shot I gave myself was sending a compound intended to strengthen my weak neurons and nodes. Here is the clever part. To get to the targeted area, the mental games were used to generate bio-electro flashes in areas of brain matter that were receiving information to be stored in short term memory. That data likely moved to long term, milliseconds later. These flashes possess a charge that act as a magnet to certain substances. The minerals in our compound have the opposite charge and are drawn specifically to the firing neurons. The proteins that are bonded to the minerals come along for the ride and eventually hook up with the neurons. I can thank Evelyn Yiki, our resident neurologist for that breakthrough theory, which at the time was a huge leap of faith.

The impulses from the various electrodes attached to me were set at the same wave amplitude as my own and resonated with and in turn amplified my own presumed weak signals. Stronger flashes made better targets for the compounds.

This experience proved be very different from the first. Almost immediately I felt warmth above the neck. It was hard to tell whether it was coming from the cap or the skull itself. A buzzing sensation came from the electrodes but not emanating from each individual contact. Rather they had merged into one hard to localize feeling starting in the lower abdomen, then pulsing up through the chest.

The neuron mixture was taking a different path. I could tell its direction from the coolness in my veins. If it was going to my brain, it wasn't taking the shortest route. It was fanning out in several directions at once.

If it was possible to know fear and exhilaration in the same event, this was it. The possibility was that what I was doing might have a bad outcome or on the other hand prove we were on the verge of a huge breakthrough. Either way it was too late to turn back.

Soon I developed a low grade headache, a slight case of nausea and sporadic hot chills. It took great effort to ignore these but I had to remain focused on the mental tasks so as not to jeopardize the procedure. The twenty minutes seemed like hours.

It must have been near the end of the experiment when a sudden brightness occurred. It was not a hot flash. More like an intensifying of the light in the room.

And then the computer beeped three times and the monitor read 'Sequence Complete'. I didn't immediately remove the CommCap or electrodes. I took a moment to self-assess my condition and see if anything in me hurt. In general, I was ok. The side effects were gone but I was a little disappointed. I guess I expected more noticeable changes. Stick to the plan I told myself. It was too early for results.

The one thing I did notice was a heightened awareness of my surroundings. Little things like the pair of pecan colored wood entrance doors, a flickering fluorescent light ready to burn out, empty oxygen tanks stockpiled by the exit doors, open beakers of chemicals on top of storage cabinets and computer screens sitting raised on stacks of paper. I talked to Ty later about housekeeping in the lab.

On the operations that followed, I made a few adjustments to the work plan. The intensity of the CommCap signals were dialed back, the dosage of the protein cocktail was reduced and the procedure time was cut back by five minutes. When all the sessions were completed Ty independently analyzed the results and confirmed what I already knew. The treatments were successful.

I was absorbing a lot more information and able to retrieve it with ease. Dates, times and tasks were no longer hidden in my mental purgatory. For example, I remember what I ate three weeks ago on our family night out. Chicken MooGoo Gao Pan at Yai Pai Moor's Tuesday night.

Other people noticed a change in me as well. Kelly, the kids, the team. Even Lars said something to the effect 'I can't put my finger on it but there is something different about you.' Inwardly I laughed when they asked if it was my hair. Only one other person knew what it was.

And so I returned to the office routine knowing that our research was paying off, professionally and personally. Mindco could make products that would revolutionize enhancing the human brain.

There are a couple of side issues I am still dealing with. I am hoping by listening to these recordings later I can objectively determine if I am undergoing any real changes that are too subtle for anyone to observe.

First of all, it is not just my short term memory that's better, my long term is as well. It is detailed, vivid and goes way back. I am seeing places and situations I didn't previously remember. I don't seek them out. They spontaneously invade my train of thought throughout the day. Ordinarily I would say that I am reliving moments from the past, but I honestly don't think I was consciously aware of them at the time. This is the first I am recalling those moments. Several of them bring me sadness. Times that Kelly and the kids spoke to me and I was off in another world. Now I can almost hear their speech word for word, followed by my silence. Those seemingly innocuous but precious opportunities of connection are lost today. Even though I still have everyone to more fully enjoy, there is a cloud of melancholy that hopefully will dissipate.

Social/psychological sciences speak of selective perception: we only see whats important to us, suggesting that is what our neurons store. I think differently now. I believe it all enters our head and it is stored there until we selectively retrieve what we want through gates that open to varying degrees. My gates have just been made wider. Very little is held back, including the good and the bad.

I know that person I am remembering has vanished, but I didn't realize until now the full extent of who he was. It is also not clear either whether the changes from this process will continue some sort transformation in me. The source eludes me right now, but internally I feel a definite shift of perspective. I still enjoy my work, but I don't feel the same frantic urgency to finish my tasks or solve some of the issues in our studies. Frankly, some days I'm in no hurry to go into work at all.

Our trade assumes that every new invention will have its glitches that are discovered later and have to be corrected. In my case I hope they are minor. Either way, I believe I am a better person to myself and those around me, even if there prove to be a few tradeoffs."

Peter's cell phone rings and Kelly's profile appears on the screen.

"I need to take this call. Signing off on session one. Session two to resume next week."

NURSE SPEAK

It isn't where you came from, it's where you're going that counts.

ELLA FITZGERALD

The Taylor Anderson Regional Memorial Center for Life was built on the site of the old Harrison Park tenements. Sitting on eight city blocks in downtown Los Angeles, with a bed capacity of 4,000, it was the largest hospital in the U.S. It had no intention of competing to be the biggest, but the State of California had no choice. The soaring costs of medical care and the surges in immigrant and elderly populations created a tipping point. The system of decentralized hospitals and clinics with all its duplications and inefficiencies was near collapse. The state took the bold step of developing this one stop shop super hospital, or Mega-Med as the media called it.

Chelsea Gregg looked up in wonder at the 10 story glass and sandstone structure as she stepped off the express bus. How lucky she was to land her first job fresh out of nursing school at this brand new state-of-the-facility. She set her senses on high alert to absorb everything she could this first week as well as to ensure she didn't say something stupid.

She entered the grand lobby and approached the security/reception desk in the center. After presenting her driver's license and access letter, an escort was summoned to transport her to Human Resources on the fifth floor. There she was issued a name badge, security card, watched a video about the mission of the Center for Life and filled out a slew of benefits forms. She had been trained on medical software in school so it came as a surprise that paperwork was still alive and well.

Next she sat in a waiting area with a dozen other new hires. Eventually a nurse hurried in and introduced herself.

"Hi, you're Chelsea? I'm Nancy Rale your Center Guide. I'll show you around then we'll go to the unit you are assigned to."

"Pleased to meet you, Nancy. I'm excited to be here and can't wait to get started."

They walked out together and started their trek around the complex.

"This was a good time for you to start. Normally new hires are put on evening shift to give the veterans a break. We just don't have enough personnel for the day shifts. Hospitals are still hurting from the nursing shortage."

"Either way is fine. I am happy to finally start my

career. I want to do some good."

Nancy was moving at a brisk pace. Her muscular calves gave evidence to many years on the floor. Chelsea was young and considered herself reasonably fit from her own regular workouts, but she had to nearly trot to keep up.

"We'll only cover the highlights today. By all rights, this should be a three-day tour, but we don't have any spare time to allow us to be off-line that long. Over time you'll learn as you go by working each unit."

"Each unit?" Chelsea asked.

"Yes, even though you will have a home base, from time to time you will support other areas as well."

They came to a bridge that connected two buildings. Beneath them was an interior atrium plush with tropical plants. Chirping bird sounds flowed from speakers hidden in the plants.

Nancy continued, "We're leaving block 1, the Admin wing. Ahead is the Pediatrics Block. Then Cancer, Heart, Gastronomic-Intestinal, Surgical, Geriatrics and Therapy-Recovery. Eight blocks in all. Each block breaks further down into specialty disciplines within. The plan was to have a full complement of staff trained and experienced in each discipline dedicated to each block. That hasn't materialized yet. Again, the nurse shortage problem. That's why we move people between areas"

"Doesn't that get confusing?"

"Well the good news is you learn a ton and you gain a broad perspective."

Nancy then leaned toward Chelsea's ear, cupped her hand, and half-whispered, "Of course the downside is we don't always know what we are doing. You just have to learn to pretend like you know."

That sounded a bit strange to Chelsea, but decided it was nothing more than casual conversation.

The birthing center was in this wing. About twenty individual rooms flanked a plain corridor. Chelsea stuck her head into an empty one expecting to find a no-nonsense plain white room with a one or maybe two adjustable beds. What she saw was a real homelike bedroom laid out before her. The double bed and night stand were metal but veneered to look like dark cherry. The two plush chairs facing the bed were upholstered in a bright patterned fabric matching the oriental rug. Paintings of landscapes decorated the walls. Instead of a boxy TV hung from the ceiling, a flat screen was inset into a cherry finished shelving unit.

"Very nice," Chelsea commented. "Not what I'm used to seeing in a patient room. Is the delivery room nearby? At the last place I interned it was on another floor."

Amused by Chelseas surprise, Nancy answered, "This is it. The delivery takes place right here."

"Really?!" she said in disbelief.

"The mothers love it. In some cases, it is more like home than home is. Reduces stress and there is a higher percentage of successful deliveries. Of course we don't want moms getting too comfortable. The lights are programmed to get harsher after delivery and the meals plainer. The goal is to have them happy to be here but happier to leave."

They continued on and turned down another corridor. Along the way the solid wall turned into 20 feet of floor to ceiling windows. Here Nancy waved her card at the door, it unlocked and they entered. The room was obviously the nursery as it was filled cribs and resting infants. Chelsea immediately noted they were covered in some kind of unusual insulated silver coated wrap. Odder still, it was pulsing.

Chelsea stopped at one crib and stared.

"Here is another innovation at the Center for Life." Nancy said. "We are able to capture and digitize the sound and timing of each mother's heartbeat. Every person has their own unique pattern, just like a fingerprint. In here it is replicated in the baby's cover, making a smoother, calmer transition from the womb to the harsh world. Gradually the stimulae are faded to zero at release."

From behind them, another nurse entered.

"Jubela," Nancy greeted.

"Danfry," the other responded.

Nancy went on, "Hi, I'm Nancy from Block 7. This is Chelsea, our latest talent we just hired. She's getting the nickel tour."

"Pleasure to meet you two. My name is Naomi Landis. Welcome to Baby Land." Naomi was short and chunky with a perpetual bright smile. The perfect personality to work in the maternity ward.

"Same here. A pleasure," Chelsea said.

Nancy took the lead. "I need to speak with Naomi a second. Have a look around." The two moved to a corner of the room.

Chelsea strolled among the cribs admiring how beauty could reside in so many forms. Spanish, Chinese, Black, White. mixed. Not an ugly one in the bunch. Behind her she could hear the two talking in low tones but could not decipher the conversation.

"Rodlow finser pock do bif safty cran. Ogber lisser Rigi krift."

"Rigid krift?"

"Chibbar, Rigi krift."

"Losonor wipsu fonarick!"

"Zaka"

Ok, now this is getting weird, Chelsea thought. She didn't feel confident enough though to question what the deal was. She just continued to wander the aisles as if everything was normal. She would have to ask later. Finally, the two veterans returned.

"The little ones are all so sweet." Chelsea began, "I can't discern the nationalities but they look like they come from a wide variety of backgrounds."

"Good observation," Naomi confirmed. "LA is already a melting pot. You add in the surrounding suburbs the Center draws from, then a broad mix is guaranteed. Many of the parents who come here can't speak English."

"That must be hard on you," Chelsea noted.

"Not too bad. The Center has two people on staff who speak four languages each. We can go to them in case of emergency," Naomi said.

"It's starting to sound like they have everything here," Chelsea said in amazement.

"That they do," Nancy said.

The next morning, Chelsea stepped off the elevator onto the fourth floor of Block 7, the Geriatrics wing. She had donned her new scrubs comprised of green slacks and a top printed with a forest of trees. The excitement of starting to work in earnest at the Center for Life wearing the team uniform was hard to contain.

She hurried down the all too familiar corridor of support rooms she had experienced in other medical facilities. Nothing new here. It seemed the length of a football field before she reached the patient center.

At the end it opened up into a large square space bounded by individual rooms on the outside surrounding a circular nurses station in the center. This arrangement was not unlike other places she had worked at before, only larger, maybe twice the size. Before she could take a count, she heard her name broadcast from the speakers overhead.

"Nurse Gregg, please report to Room 401."

She looked back and saw a glass wall behind the counter. Nancy was behind it, a microphone in one hand, the other waving her into the room.

Nancy pulled a chair for Chelsea while five other nurses turned from their work at the counters. Chelsea faintly blushed.

"I didn't mean to scare you. Thought you would enjoy hearing your name announced over the system. Let me introduce you to our group. Starting on your left we have Marci, then Adrian, Tamika, Janice and Sandra."

"Pleasure to meet you," Chelsea said self-consciously.

"Tell us a little something about yourself," Marci asked.

"I grew up in Tulare County, just outside of Visalia. Went to Nursing School in Bakersfield where I just graduated. I always wanted to be a nurse, so this a wonderful opportunity for me. I would eventually like to become a nurse practitioner so hopefully what I learn here will help."

Janice inserted, "You certainly came to the right place. School is great for the medicine part, and learning what new trends may come from research. But here you see how a hospital really runs and how things get done. We'll help you with that."

"That's why you're here," Nancy added. "You will meet the other floor nurses later. Right now, it was best for you to be connected to our group first. This team will be your mentors. Any time you have a question ask them"

Tamika chimed in, "Right. We know how to work around some of the roadblocks you might encounter. Also who you can work with and who to avoid."

"We jokingly call ourselves the Renal Raiders," said Nancy.

"Is there a procedures manual I can read up on in my spare time?" Chelsea asked.

"Spare time?!" Sandra laughed. "I haven't heard

that term in ages."

"OK ladies. Let's not scare the help away the first day here." Nancy interjected. "Yes, there is a manual you can look at but it won't help much. To many changes around here. It is outdated in many parts. There is also some stuff you'll need to know that can't be written down."

"I understand."

"We need to get back to work. Adrian, why don't you walk Chelsea around the floor. Show her where everything is and how the new equipment works."

As the two walked out of the room, Marci and Tamika could be heard saying, "Mongho ri gere."

"Tai. Tai."

They both laughed.

First stop was the supply room. It was filled with row after row of ceiling high shelving containing bedpans, catheters, crutches, braces, plastic gloves and the like.

"This is big. I'm used to a small closet on each floor. Does this serve the whole block?"

"Nope, just the floor. You may have noticed the large number of patient rooms back there."

"As a matter of fact I did."

"You'd be surprised, but we go through a lot of product for those old folks. The initial concept was that a large supply room on each floor would mean less lost time running to another wing or waiting for replenishment. It would make us more product-ive. Looked good on paper but there were still problems. There are shortages that were miscalculated and since they down-sized the procurement unit, materials we need can be hard to get."

"Doesn't that effect patient care?" Chelsea asked, concerned.

"Normally it would. Fortunately, we've found a couple of ways around it. One is we share resources between the blocks. You'll meet one today. We need you to go over to Block Four in a few minutes to pick up a supply of dressings. I'll give you a name and room number. Just say Jubela and she'll understand."

"I'll be happy to go, but I don't quite understand. Is there some secrecy involved here?"

"Nancy will lay it all out for you later. We forged a network across the campus to move 'stock' as we call it. It's not an open network so this has to be kept low key. Again, Nancy will fill in the details."

They continued down the service corridor arriving at a door controlled by a keypad. Adrian punched in the code. Inside three young men were sitting at a console of computer screens.

"Here is the most advanced feature of the Center. When you hear the name Mensa Station, this is it. All of the patients in this block are monitored here. The other blocks have a similar station. Data is then sent out to the nurse's station, the nurses themselves and the doctors. The doctors can even consult with each other over treatments, then issue instructions back to the nurse's station."

"Does that change what the doctors do here."

"Yes, it means they don't have to come in as often.

And it saves money for the physician, the Center and the insurance company."

"Doesn't the doctor need to physically see and examine the patient?"

"Not like they used to. Here's something the public is not aware of yet: Technology can now detect and interpret more than doctors can. Think about it. When you go to their office, what do they do? Check your temperature and look down your throat. How primitive is that? And the interview is worthless too. People distort or otherwise miss-communicate their symptoms and habits. This is way more accurate."

"How about the patients? Don't they expect to talk face to face with their physician?"

"Yes, that has been a problem. There have been complaints of being left in the dark. We're working on that too. Trying out something called an MSA or Medical Services Advisor. They wear the white coat, meet directly with the patient or guardian, and present themselves like an expert with results scripted for them by the doctor or lab technician. We're trying it in Block 7 first since the seniors are less likely to question or push back."

Chelsea ran the errand to Block Four and returned with the lot of dressings. It had felt awkward to say the odd word but it did meet with a warm response. The other nurse gave her an extensive background on the unit and offered her any assistance that might help her acclimation. She had anticipated a lengthy learning curve for an organization of this magnitude, and it still could be. She was feeling a general sense of acceptance though. Even if she still didn't totally understand everything she encountered at the moment, at least her team would get her through.

Back at Block Seven it was Sandra's turn to be the guide. "Let's drop in on some of our guests." she said leading the way along one side. In the first few rooms, the patients were dozing, perhaps from medication. In the third, an elderly woman lay in bed half inclined reading a magazine about cooking. She looked up and smiled as the two entered.

Sandra spoke in a hushed tone. "Panliare rushkue. Oops, I mean hip surgery. Her second time in. First she had a knee replacement. The other knee gave out and she fell and broke her hip. She's also hard of hearing so we have to speak up."

"Mrs. Snyder, how are you today?" Sandra said loudly.

"I'm doing ok for now. Pain comes back when I stay in one position for a while. I may need something for that later."

"We'll keep an eye on it."

"Who is the young lady with you today?"

"This is Nurse Gregg. She'll be working with us from now on."

"What is your first name?"

"Chelsea."

"Leslie, what a nice name."

"Chelsea! Her name is Chelsea," Sandra shouted, with a noticeable edge of irritation.

"Oh, Chelsea. How lovely. You remind me of my granddaughter. Would you mind sitting here for a moment so I could learn a little bit about you?"

Chelsea started for the side chair when Sandra touched her arm to stop her.

"We need to check your progress, Mrs. Snyder," Sandra said, as she lifted up the covers to look over the site of the surgery. "Chelsea, you can check her IV. See if any of the meds are near depletion."

"There's a scrumptious chicken gumbo recipe in here. Would the Center mind if I keep it?" Mrs. Snyder asked.

"Not at all."

"Should I check her chart?" Chelsea asked.

Sandra went soft. "That's another advancement. No more charts. Everything's on the pad. Here, have a look at her profile. Condition, meds, vitals. All there. All you need to do is confirm you checked in and make sure the equipment is functioning as it should be."

Chelsea studied the data. "Will I be giving her these medications?"

"Yes. but I'll go over that with you later." Sandra lay the covers back in place. "You're mending nicely, Mrs. Snyder. Keep doing it." She then went over to a small marker board on the wall and wrote Chelsea's name in place of hers. "Nurse Gregg will be your regular day nurse." She then led the two to the door.

"Nice meeting you, Leslie. Please come back. If my son or granddaughter are waiting outside, you can send them in." the patient said with expectation.

Without looking back, Sandra rolled her eyes and replied. "We certainly will do."

Once out of range she admonished Chelsea. "One thing you have to be careful of is to not let the patient draw you into becoming their surrogate family. Sad to say but most here don't have visitors. Their next of kin may live cross country, are busy with their own families or work, are deceased, or just simply don't care. Those that do stop in keep it brief."

"I guess I wasn't aware of anything unusual from her. She seemed like she was just being friendly," Chelsea said defensively.

"She was. We're trained to take care of them physically, not mentally or emotionally. That's someone else's job. In this section alone, we have fifty beds to cover with one round an hour, not counting situations that occur in between. That means we're expected to cover the floor efficiently. And we're not on the honor system. The device I showed you tracks our rounds each day. How long did we stay in each room, how many beds did we cover and what tasks were completed? Our performance scores are based on it which ultimately determines our raises."

"I didn't realize."

"Oh, I wouldn't expect you too. The Center has implemented many things you won't find anywhere else. Brave New Hospital."

"Now I'm not feeling as prepared as I thought I was. I should be more cautious."

Sandra quickly reassured, "Don't worry. You'll be fine. You're set with us."

They moved briskly through their rounds, finishing their checks just before lunch. Sandra had been right. There was a cloud of forlorn that hung over these patients. Not one visitor on the floor. At least the thought of helping these seniors through their health problems prevented the experience from being a complete wipeout.

"Any plans for lunch?" Sandra asked.

"I brought a salad and yogurt. I haven't figured out the eating spots around here yet."

"Salad and yogurt. A right proper meal for a hospital employee to eat. Why don't you leave it in the fridge and join us in the cafeteria?"

"I'd like that. Where at?"

"It's on the roof of Block Three. Our group usually sits in an area called Tom Cruise."

-

The cafeteria of the Taylor Anderson Center for Life occupied the entire roof of Block Three. One quarter kitchen, one quarter servery and one half dining area. The seating area was bathed in daylight from skylights and full height windows around the perimeter. The building wasn't a high-rise, but the panorama views of LA were still impressive.

The pattern of columns divided the enormous space into sections which the clusters of tables helped reinforce. Capitalizing on the regional presence of Hollywood, each section contained supergraphic banners of movie stars hung from the high ceiling. Tom Hanks, Meryl Streep, George Clooney, and oldies like Clark Gable and Elizabeth Taylor were displayed in iconic scenes from their films.

Chelsea took a while navigating the myriad of food choices and struggled to make a decision. She went with chicken stir fry and after paying, easily picked out a scene from Top Gun among the banners. Janice saw her, stood up and waved her over to the group.

Marci and Adrian were in a heated discussion.

"Hist talon Tamar waddorap dilaned."

"Azuse farg."

"Farg di bufdi."

Chelsea couldn't contain her puzzlement any longer. "If you don't mind my asking, what are you two speaking?"

"We do need to get you up to speed on our special vocabulary." Nancy said. "It's unique to our group. Let me explain."

"Don't be obvious, but see those nurses at the next table? Try to listen to their conversation." Chelsea listened.

["Ese nuevo medico dirigido rojo en cask de emergencia es Lindo."]

["Se pero tiene un anillo."]

"I can hear them talking but can't make out their words. It sounds like they're speaking Spanish. I don't speak it so I can't make out their words," Chelsea guessed.

"They are. I don't speak it either. For the longest time it bugged the hell out of me. Their chatter would start out in English, then slide into Spanish, then bounce back and forth after that. It felt like they were deliberately shielding their talk from English speaking ears. And it's not only at that table. You'll find that all over the dining hall. In the Tom Hanks section, you have the doctors, most of whom are Indian and some Chinese. In the Julia Roberts section are the orderlies. They're Mexican and Vietnamese. Nurses fill up several areas. African American, white, and mixtures from the middle east. Each in their own little circle."

Chelsea looked around the hall. "I see what you mean. Judging from what I saw in the nursery, and the mixed neighborhoods around here, I shouldn't be surprised."

Nancy went on. "Exactly. And the Center promotes diversity. For me, I'm fine with it. My beef is when we talk, we can't relax in our own little world. When we want to have our own private little talk that no one else needs to hear, our speech is understood by anyone and everyone.

Then it came to us. Why not invent our own language? Come up with words that no one will understand, except for our little team. So we did exactly that, and are still working on it. It's fun. Each of us tries to create a word, particularly for situations where we need to be discreet."

"So do you have something like a dictionary written down. I'd like to study it as I get time." Chelsea asked.

"No, it's an immersive verbal language, not written. Besides, it still is evolving. And what started out as a social game for us soon revealed useful benefits for our work. There are some things the patients don't need to hear us saying. There are also some staff that aren't on the best terms with us and we don't trust. So conversing in this way will be important for you to learn. But again, we're here to help. We'll practice with you at lunch and on breaks. There are only a few patterns that we follow. For instance, some new names have been assigned to others we work with. To protect the guilty. 'Vapor' stands for Nurse Parker. She's the nursing manager for our building. You haven't met her yet and may not for quite a while. Meetings and reports have her buried, so we rarely see her. That's a good thing because we can get things done our way without being micro-managed.

And then there is 'Gonzo'. It's our name for Dr. Randalla. He breezes through once a week as if he's late for a golf date. Very arrogant and gives the staff a hard time.

For efficiency, some phrases are condensed or represent different words depending on the sentence. Like 'wi' for 'was a' or 'was the', 'ti' for 'to a' or 'to the', or 'bi' for 'be a' or 'be the' and so on. For no reason in particular, animals may mean good or bad, like 'herford' for 'jerk'. Beef jerky. Get the association?"

It took a second, but eventually Chelsea did. She nodded.

"So when you hear, 'Gonzo bi heffer' it means 'Dr. Randalla is a jerk.'"

The other women laughed.

"I could go on all day but we need to finish lunch.

That's our non-English lesson for today." Another group ha-ha.

Chelsea glanced around the ceiling as she ate her lunch. She tried guessing the actors' names and the movies from which the scenes were taken. In keeping with the Center for Life, some were obviously medical plots. Every actor must have played a doctor: Robin Williams, Eddie Murphy, George C. Scott, William Hurt. Same for nurses: Renee Zellweger, Jacklyn Smith, Sally Kellerman, Emma Thompson and Audrey Hepburn. Straight ahead she saw Whoopy Goldberg in Scrubs. She stared and wondered: Hospitals are nothing like the movies.

Two weeks later, Chelsea was completing the rounds on her own. She had a basic understanding of the building geography and could find her way around the mega-campus. The tips she received from her home team helped her settle into a routine quickly.

In college, she excelled at learning and remembering the elaborate Latin names for medications and the anatomy. With that skill she was able to absorb the group's lingo. She just considered it a second language.

"Good morning, Mr. Brickler," Chelsea said. The balding man in bed slowly opened one eye, then with great effort, the other. Though still groggy from a sedative, he forced out some words. "Where is the nearest smoking lounge?".

"Sorry, Sir. It's closed for repairs."

"There isn't a smoking lounge, is there?"

Not looking at the patient, she continued checking the monitors and IV while simultaneously ticking off tasks on her tablet. "No, sir. There isn't."

"Crazy rule. No cigarettes in a hospital," he grumbled.

"Mr. Brickler. You just had most of one lung removed. I don't think you want to ruin the other. That goes, you go."

"Thanks for the advice young lady," he was able to say, before having a coughing fit. It was obvious that made him hurt. "Ooh! Aw! I thought the surgery would fix me."

She brought a dixie cup of water and a small basin over for him to rinse and spit out fluid. "It will take some time for you to heal. You'll be glad later."

He groaned, deciding not to temp the spasm again by talking.

She made a slight adjustment to the pain medication. Checking her watch, she confirmed she was making her rounds in good time. This afternoon she hoped to better her time.

Nancy met Chelsea at the door as she was leaving. "Fi dooca?"

['Any problems?'] Nancy asked in a low tone.

"Mip. Heemer bi chanivar Jayco."

['No. He's not a happy camper,'] Chelsea replied.

"Bu trollab. Heenin prut o li bitzy upter erka ti bi sing tawa leuta. Ti seeding er mallidine, ker ti heenin mang locknin."

['It's understandable. His good lung is only marginally better than the one that was removed. The outlook is bad but it's his own undoing.']

"I can hear you," Mr. Brickler uttered weakly. "I don't know what that gibberish is you're spouting, but it had better not be about me."

"Not to worry, sir," Nancy returned. "Just going over some official business." Then continuing with Chelsea. "Dy mallidine. Ti shang heener slank bumben. Rarch."

['Too bad. I give him five more years. Tops.']

"yi phaxa."

['So sad.']

They moved out of the room. Nancy was about to say something when they heard a man yell from the other end of the hall.

"Why isn't someone coming. My back is killing me. My buzzer's broken."

"That's because we turned it off at the front desk," Nancy confided softly to Chelsea.

"I can go see what he wants," Chelsea offered.

"No, don't. He's a shouter. Once in a while we get someone who is habitually agitated. Nothing suits them. They ring their button non-stop as if they're the only one here."

"Maybe it's serious."

Nancy pointed to Chelsea's tablet.

"See that square marked PQ. It stands for pain quotient. It's a new feature only we have. The Mensa Station reads sensors on the patient. In combination with other readings, an algorithm can determine if pain is really there. 0 means none. 10 means excruciating. See? A zero. He doesn't need any attention at the moment. We have a more important issue right now. Follow me."

Nancy walked them both up a back fire stair to the floor above. The hallway they entered was dim, lit only by emergency lighting. No one else was passing through suggesting it was a service wing. Nancy knocked once then twice on the first door they came to. A lock clicked then the door opened and Tamika greeted them. The large room they entered had no finished ceiling and the walls were unpainted. Its use was obviously for dead storage, meant as a temporary holding space for equipment already outmoded by advances in technology. Sensors, microscopes, scanners and fat blank computer screens were scattered everywhere.

All of the Renal Raiders were present and accounted for.

Nancy began. "Marci, why don't you start with an update?"

"Sure, our friend in chemo overheard Nurse Ralston's bragging to a resident. Seems she sees herself as head nurse over all the units, not just the Cancer Block. She has been maneuvering to make a name for herself. Getting profiles about herself put in the newsletter. Talking about how there is so much more potential for staff improvement with the right leadership. Inflating the performance levels of her group."

"I'm hearing the same thing," Janice added. "I have a friend who is the admin to Ralston's boss, Director Frank Egan. She saw a memo from Ralston to Frank promoting the idea of consolidating all the nursing units under him."

Nancy followed. "He's the type to suck the idea up. It would mean more power for him and she likely would get a promotion. It would be terrible for us. First off, she would slowly but surely replace us with her friends. Raises and choice hours? Forget it. They would selectively go to her closest allies. Nope, we need to stop her in her tracks. Quick!"

Weeks before she would have been too timid to speak up, but now feeling part of the group Chelsea voiced her reservations. "There isn't a whole lot we can do, is there? Our influence is limited to our unit."

"We have been through this many, many times before," Nancy answered confidently. "Consider it a normal part of surviving in a large institution. Isn't that right ladies?" They all nodded. "First thing we to do is counter her self-promotion campaign with one of our own. We need to find out what's wrong with her area. I've heard they have issues. Let's find them. Janice and Marci, why don't you two have lunch with your friends there and see what gripes they have. Get specifics and list any staff willing to vent their frustrations. We can help them file a grievance with their union rep."

Sandra offered a contribution. "I can work with the guys at the Mensa Station and look for discrepancies between her PR garbage and the actual performance records of her unit. I am sure there are some."

Adrian joined in. "Customer complaints would

be good to catch her up on. There is a surprising amount of scoring sites, including Federal, on the Internet. Nothing hurts more than public criticism."

"Oh, that's a good one. Adrian. We also need to keep Ralston busy. Get a bunch of paperwork thrown her way. Tamika, contact our union steward, Pat Doland. I'm sure she'll help. She won't want to see our membership reduced. Tell Pat what's going on and see what extra forms can be thrown at Ralston to complete."

Nancy then looked at Chelsea, rubbing her chin in thought. "I really hate to involve you, but we need everyone's effort on this."

"Oh, no problem. Please include me. This affects me as well. What can I do to help?" Chelsea volunteered.

"It's all about networking and alliances. The more loyal partners we have, the better. We need more contacts in Blocks 2 and 5. I'll give you a few names to get started."

"I'd be happy to do it. I'm all in."

"Wonderful." Nancy summed up for the others. "I have a bridge party in two weeks with some Center for Lifers. We all used to worked together at LA General before it was closed and we were transferred here. One of them is a Human Resources Director and a close friend. Give me what you find before then and I'll bend her ear at the game. Enough said. Let's get back before someone questions our absence."

They all hugged, then returned back from different directions so as not to raise suspicion.

The following Saturday evening, Chelsea was multi-tasking in the kitchenette of her small studio apartment. She was reading a journal article on medicine interactions and at the same time cooking spaghetti when her cell phone rang. It was in her purse, so she turned down the heat and ran into the living room. Why is it the darned thing always manages to sink to the bottom every time? After fumbling it out she answered before the call dropped.

"Middue. Croben ravor?" she said without thinking.

A brief pause from the caller. "What? I'm sorry. Must have the wrong number. I was trying for Chelsea Gregg."

Realizing her mistake, she shifted to recovery mode. "Polly, is that you?!"

"Oh, uh hi Chelsea. Yes, it's me. For a second there, I couldn't make out what you said. We must have a bad connection."

"No, to be honest, I was lost in thought about work. Some office jargon slipped out."

Polly Hagen was Chelsea's best friend from Visalia. They grew up together and graduated from the same nursing school.

"I was watching to see if you'd stop back or call. Thought we might go out for pizza or a movie. It's been a little while since we last talked, so I thought I'd call and catch up."

"My goodness, I'm glad you did. How are you? Where did you land? In a hospital?", Chelsea asked.

"No. Not many open positions around here. Most facilities have cut back. A lot of services were transferred down your way to the Center of Life. Finally got a job at a nursing home. Not what I envisioned starting out, but the pay is decent. Can't complain."

"That's great. I'm working with the elderly as well," Chelsea said as she worked her way back to the stove.

"What's going on with you? How's life in the big city?" Polly asked.

"Not what I expected either, but in a good way. I'm learning a lot. Being challenged with something different every day. Working extra hours but I can use the extra pay. Working with a great group of nurses. They're helping me a lot get into their groove. They treat me like family. Working for a big hospital is way more complicated than what you and I learned in school. I would be lost without them."

"You are braver than I am. I couldn't deal with both LA and a big place like that. Are you coming back to Tulare soon, maybe next weekend? I miss hanging out with you. Maybe we could cruise Bakersfield for fun like we used to."

While adding a little garlic to the pot, Chelsea had glanced down at the journal and lost track of the conversation. The silence made her realize it was her turn to respond. "I'm sorry Polly. I get lousy reception in this building. What was that last part?"

"Are you coming back any time soon? Frankly, I miss you being here."

"Miss you too. I can't say right now exactly when I'll return. I do need to get back and pick up a few things at the house but I'm still in the middle of getting settled. At work and in the neighborhood. Do you ever get down this way?"

"You know I'm a country girl. Nothing appealing to me about LA to make me want to visit the city except the fact that you're there. I suppose if you can give me a good day to come I could make the trip."

Chelsea turned the page, turned off the stove, and spooned a helping of spaghetti onto a plate. "That would be great. Let me think about it and get back to you."

"Chelsea, one other thing," Polly said more seriously.

"What is that?"

"Your mother called me."

"She did? What did she want?"

"Just to talk I guess. She hadn't heard from you since you moved. Wanted to know if I knew if there was anything wrong with you. Of course I said I didn't know."

"Hopefully you can see, I mean tell, that I am ok," she answered defensively.

"It sounds like it. Would you like me to call her back and reassure her?"

"No, that is really something I should do. I haven't been very diligent in checking in at home. Thanks. I'll take care it."

"I know you said you are busy, so I'd better run along."

"Well thanks for calling. Good luck on your new job."

"Same to you. Bye."

"Bye."

With that, Chelsea closed the call, carried her plate of food into the dinette and said to herself:

"Ramdeller, Polly, ramdeller alinkny."

WANTED: BY ALL

*A person should design the way he makes a living
around how he wishes to make a life.*

CHARLIE BYRD

"Vern! Vern! Vern! Vern! Go Vern!" the crowd chanted endlessly.

What sounded like a college chugging contest was actually an office retirement party. Vernon Stades was at the center of it all attempting to down enough chili peppers to beat his last record at Hot Poncho's Tex-Mex Grill in downtown Atlanta, Georgia.

About 30 of Vern's friends and co-workers from WealthTrust Financial Services were encouraging him on, even though he was turning pink and had broken into a sweat. He had managed to keep up with his younger counterparts at work and the chili marathon was no exception. He could match anyone -- spice for spice.

Vern was the last veteran leaving the company. His departure meant the mean age would fall below 30. The corporation had adopted a policy of hiring the youngest and the brightest which was successfully taking root across the board. The sense of empowerment for this young generation that had been building for months crystalized in this otherwise casual afternoon get together. Their future and that of the company was totally in their hands.

A cheer erupted when the final pepper went down. Vern belched, then reached for his mug of ale while the group took turns congratulating him. Tom Dabel waited to be last so he could speak with the guest of honor at length. When it was his turn they hugged.

Tom was the first to speak. "You're finally doing it. I thought you would be here forever. Maybe WealthTrust would cast you in bronze and stand you up on a podium in the front plaza for all to admire."

"And here I thought you had a head on your shoulders. Guess you never really know who you're working with," Vern joked. "Nope, I bought a small shanty along the coast to start spending my investment savings. I've had enough of meeting earnings targets here."

"I know what you mean," which he did since he worked in the same department. "Say, I couldn't let you go without giving you a little something," he said, handing him a small gift-wrapped package.

Vern opened it to find a bottle of anti-acid tablets. He placed his right hand over his heart, looked up at the ceiling, and gave a feigned sniffle. "I'm overcome with joy."

"I knew we would be here, so I figured you would need those."

"This is so precious. Wait, I've got this wrong," he said, moving his hand from his heart to his bloated belly. "Here is where I really need them."

Tom turned serious. "All kidding aside, I wish you all the best. You've done so much for me. You'll be sorely missed and I'm not sure how I can do it without you." Vern had been something of a mentor and Tom had become dependent on his guidance.

"Aw, now you're getting mushy. You will do just fine. I saw much potential in you the moment you started which is why I invested extra time to help you along. There's plenty more adjustments you'll have to make, but I tried to give you a solid foundation. It will involve some sacrifices which can lead to several promotions. I believe in you kid."

A young woman joined them and placed her arm through Tom's. "It's time for me to take my man back."

Lacey and Tom had been going steady for the past year. She worked in the Finance Department at WealthTrust. They had frequent contact from which a relationship blossomed.

"Lacey, how are you doing today?" Vern said.

"Doing fine. Wonderful party for a great guy. Hope you won't be a stranger but I'll understand if we don't see you here again," she said warmly.

"I just told Tom about my new digs. You're both welcome to come over anytime."

"We just may take you up on it?" She looked up at Tom. "Well, must go. Time to make the next party."

At first he was surprised but then took the hint. They all embraced, shared one last round of cheers and farewells, then departed. Before Tom and Lacey could reach the exit, Egan Smith jumped up from a nearby table and intercepted them.

Egan shared a fist bump with Tom then said, "Are you going to make the Braves game next Wednesday? We've got the corporate skybox at Turner Field reserved for our group and the team has started off the season great. 6 and 2 so far."

"I'll definitely be there. It'll be fun. I'm bringing Lacey." She squeezed his arm.

"Of course. She's part of our pack."

"Just make sure there is enough food."

"Oh, there will be. Don't forget about this Saturday either. We have a company softball game out at Pittman Park. We need you at first base. I sent a text to Alex Rimes in Accounting that we planned to whoop them in the first inning."

"I haven't forgotten," Tom replied with a smile but kept on moving so that he and Lacey could escape. "See you there." he shouted back as they passed through the door."

Tom and Lacey were a popular couple. He was tall, good looking and stood out in most crowds. His Turkish genes gave him deep black hair and dark eyes possessing a dashing flair. A special knack for numbers and budgets made him something of a rising star and those around him sensed he was destined for bigger things.

There probably is a study somewhere confirming that tall people and short people have a natural affinity for each other. Lacey was a petite, attractive but sharp red-head who monitored the portfolios that came from Tom. They hit it off immediately. Compared to other corporations, WealthTrust had a fairly relaxed policy on office relationships. If it didn't interfere with work, and one party did not report directly to the other, nothing was said.

Adding to the mix was their affable personalities which put them on the invitation lists for many afterhours socials. So much so, it was a challenge to find time for just themselves.

They walked two blocks back to headquarters and went behind the building to the landscaped break area that faced Conklin Street. It was a lush employee amenity that no one ever used so it made a perfect place to sit and talk without fear of interruption.

"Oh my goodness. The noise is still ringing in my ears," she said, holding her hands over her ears. "I love the peace and quiet here."

"Our group does get rowdy, but they do know how to have fun."

"They sure do. And we're lucky to have such a great group of friends. It would be good though to make some of our own fun."

"Uhuh," he replied.

"We didn't make it out the door without committing more of our evenings."

"I know," he answered blandly, nervous about where the conversation was leading.

"It sure would be nice if we could take off somewhere together, just you and me. Don't you think?" Lacey pleaded, touching his arm.

"It would. I know it's been a hassle. Right now, I'm reaching a point where I think I'll get more responsibility. With Vern's retirement there will be a lot of reshuffling. I have a shot at a big move up. Going to these parties and games gets me in solid with the group and hopefully boosts my recognition."

"And I want to see that happen too. But there's no reason why we can't make this work for us as well. Don't you want that too?"

"Of course I do," Tom reassured.

"Then we need to do something about it. I brought up an idea a while back and now I think it's the only way, given our current situation. We should move in together. It's a big step, I know, but I am totally comfortable with it. We would be building your career and our relationship at the same time. What do you say?"

"I agree. It would be terrific living together. I would have no personal hesitation to doing it except for some complications. It's just not as easy as it sounds."

"And it won't get any easier," she pressed. "The more you wait, the harder it will get. Besides, I am not sure living at home looks great from leadership's perspective. They're looking for someone who is strong and independent. Not that you aren't. It's just the appearance. You really need to move out."

"You are probably right."

"We can start looking for a place tomorrow. How about it?" she said excitedly.

"Sure. Why not. We can see what's out there at least," Tom offered.

Lacey changed her position so that she was on her knees on the bench facing Tom. "Oh this will be terrific. You'll see."

"It should be an apartment close to work. That would cut back my present drive in and give us more free time."

She put her arms around Tom and said, "I can't wait." After a few pecks on the cheek she continued. "And you're going to have to tell them at home. Soon."

"I know."

Ten years earlier, the Dabel family came to America under duress. They had lived in Babek outside of Istanbul, Turkey, not far from the Bosporus Strait. Their home was large, comfortable and noisy. Tom was the oldest of 6. Two brothers, Altan and Cemil, and 3 sisters, Paloma, Sevda, and Qiana. His grandparents lived in a small cottage along the same lane.

Tom's father, Emir Dabel, ran a successful import/export business. His wife, Irmak, managed the household, which she executed with efficiency and firmness. Both kept everything organized within well-defined roles. Being the oldest son, Tom was responsible for helping both of them, eventually giving him the skills with numbers and people that made him a valuable commodity to employers.

The political and economic climate that made Turkey so vibrant for decades also made it vulnerable to the upheaval rampant in the region. It was perfectly situated between Europe, Asia and Africa making it a natural nexus for commerce. but unfortunately also caught in the crossfire between warring neighboring states.

Eventually violence spilled over into Istanbul. Shootings and bombings became commonplace, some dangerously close to the Dabel offices in the heart of the city. Finally, when there was a possibility the family might be targeted for their status in the community, Emir and Irmak made the painful decision to escape to America.

Like many other refugees from Turkey, they were

processed into a federally designated re-settlement community in Savannah, Georgia. Despite the traumatic experience of being uprooted, the location by the Atlantic simulated the peaceful grounding they left behind at the Bosporus. While being interned, Tom accepted the option to Americanize his name from his original surname, Ziko. It was one small step he could take to blend into the new land.

Fortunately, Emir had transferred most of their financial assets to the US before leaving Babek. This provided the means to move to Atlanta and put down new roots. Emir started up his business again in the city and bought a large home in the suburb of Peachtree Corners along the Chattahoochee River. It was large enough to hold everyone and proximate to a place nearby for their grandparents, Munir and Anna.

Tom loved coming home to it, especially for being able to take an occasional stroll down to the river to decompress. The river was not as deep or wide as the Bosporus or its American counterpart, the Mississippi, but the rippling water and steep wooded banks nonetheless accepted his presence and wrapped him with a hypnotic calm.

Tonight though he would go straight in. Pulling his car around the house, Tom let out a sigh, and let himself in through the garage. Irmak was collecting the last dishes from the table. He went over to help.

"Hello mother," he said, giving her a hug.

"Mmmm. Smells good."

"It was good," she replied, with a slight edge to her tone. "You missed a good dinner."

"I know. I could smell the menta and kofta on the way in. Any left? I might have some later"

"No. All gone. I have some lakma. I'll heat them up and leave them on the table to snack on."

"You should start a TV cooking show, momma. There's French, Italian, Spanish, barbeque but no Turkish cuisine. You know all the recipes and do them so well. You could be a star!"

"Sure. Then who would cook for all of you. Everyone would starve."

"Oops. I didn't think of that. Scratch that idea."

They finished and he went into the living room. The others were either watching TV or playing board games. Emir was reading the Dunya, a Turkish financial paper he subscribed to. Later it would be the Hurriyet for general news. He abstained from reading an electronic gadget. Using computers in his business was painful enough.

"Ziko! Ziko!" Qiana yelled, hopping over Cemil who was lying on the floor in front of the TV. She grabbed Tom's hands, tugging him into the living room "Play okey with me. Please. Sevda is not very good. She cheats!"

Sevda hollered back. "Not true. You don't know the rules!" She jumped up and left. "I'm tired of this anyway. I have to do homework."

Tom knelt down by the board and took Sevda's place in the game.

Eventually all the younger siblings went to bed. Altan, his brother, went out to work on his car. Paloma, the oldest sister, was on the phone with a friend. Their grandparents had retired to their cottage earlier. That left Emir, Irmak and Tom alone in the dining room, drinking coffee and snacking on Lakma.

Emir spoke, sipping his drink and still looking down at the paper. "The auditors are coming in this week. The books need some cleaning up. Sophia is also behind on billings. Cash flow might get squeezed. I could use your help this week end."

"I can come in after lunch."

"It will take all day. Might need Sunday too."

"I have an office function in the morning. I'll stay late, if it's that bad."

Emir did not look up, but Tom could tell he was frowning.

"It's not bad. Just a lot coming due this time of month. Nothing a little help can't get us through."

They both had talks on this subject before. Tom saw the need to buy new business software to match the volume of transactions they were handling. Emir did well back in Istanbul with handshake deals. His style of work did not merge neatly with the regulatory requirements in their new land.

Irmak was next.

"Sevda needs a ride Saturday evening for her dance recital. She has to get there early to rehearse." Emir looked up from his paper.

"I'm helping Dad then. Alton or Paloma can take her."

"Paloma just got her license. I don't trust her to drive others around yet. Best she waits 6 months to get more experience." Tom knew better.

"And what about Altan?" Tom wanted to express his displeasure but he dared not agitate his father.

"Altan needs the time to job hunt. He hasn't found the right one yet. He's trying hard to find one." Tom knew better on that score as well. He had more to say about his brother but decided to change subjects.

"Ok. I'll work it in somehow." He paused.

"So Lacey and I have been talking and we..."

"You're still seeing that girl?" Irmak interrupted.

"Yes, mom. Never stopped. I like her a lot. That's what I want to talk about."

"I don't understand why you don't find a nice Turkic girl who would take care of you and give you a family. I'm sure there are many who came over here just like us. They don't have to be from Thrace or Marmara but it would be nice. Why even at the refugee lodging in Savannah we had neighbors from Anatolia who had attractive young daughters."

Emir joined in. "Ziki, I have an idea. Why don't you come with me to the next businessmen's meeting at the Kemal Center next week? The group is made up of accomplished leaders who you should get to know. Some have bragged about their families and their daughters. We could arrange a casual meeting somehow, maybe dinner. It's always good to have a strong network anyway."

"Listen dad, momma, I appreciate what you're trying to do for me, but this is something I have to do myself." Tom struggled to get the next part out. "And well, uh, I've been giving it a lot of thought and decided I need to move out. I am going to find my own place."

Irmek was stunned. "My goodness. Why would you want to leave? We're a family. Don't you like it here?"

Emir dropped his paper. In a hoarse voice he said, "Momma's right. We support each other here. Besides, you've got a roof over your head and fabulous meals. And friends who help keep our way of life together. We can talk in our own language and listen to our favorite songs." Cough. Cough. "Why give that up? What's gotten into you that you want to abandon us like this?"

"Whoa, wait a minute. You have the wrong idea. I am not relocating far away. Just need a little more privacy and learn to do some things on my own."

Irmek began processing the possible disruptions to their routine. "Who is going to pick up Sevda after her dance lessons and take Qiana to her sleep overs?"

Tom attempted to reassure. "I will still be here

for you. I love everyone in this house, including grandma and grandpa, and would do anything for them. But I don't need to be here every minute. Altan and Paloma are old enough to take on some responsibilities. It won't be long before Cemil will be driving and can do his share. I'll only be a phone call away. You'll be just fine."

Emir and Irmek weren't convinced, but Irmek got up and went to the sink to rinse off a few leftover dishes from dinner. They had a modern dishwasher, but cleaning up after a meal was a source of relaxation for her. This time it also hid a few tears that were forming.

Emir stiffened up but looked at Irmek and decided not to press the subject and distress her further. "Ok Ziko, You and I can talk about this later." He took his paper back into the living room to finish reading. Everyone retreated to their respective corners in quiet for the rest of the evening.

The next morning at work he was still troubled by how poorly the talk went with his parents the night before. He knew they would not be overjoyed by the sudden news, but the reality of it hurt him as much as them. He hadn't slept well, and the combination of fatigue and a swirling stew of thoughts was not a good state to be in while analyzing balance sheets. One missed observation could be costly. With a hyper caffeinated drink at hand, Tom struggled to keep his focus sharp.

Normally, this was the best time for him to get work done, before the rest of the office sauntered in. Not so today. A corporate-wide meeting scheduled for 10:00am was causing many to arrive early. His cubicle was just off the elevator, so it was natural for co-workers to stop by and chat about business and otherwise. Ivy Lirror and Ken Brockett were first with updates on their favorite cable shows. He watched neither but they were extremely passionate about the plot twists so he listened intently. They were followed by Egan Smith, who dropped off reports he had worked on the night before.

Finally, Lacey came in and sat down in his guest chair.

"So, how did it go?"

"Not very well. They took it hard."

She put her hand on his. "Don't worry. They'll get over it. Parents often have a hard time when their first child leaves the roost."

"With them it's going to take some time. You have to understand. Being uprooted from Babek was traumatic. Keeping the family intact was the one thing unchanged. It was our only basis of security."

"I understand. Or at least I'll try. If you keep calling on them, they will feel much better about it." Lacey pulled some papers out of her purse. "Here. This will take your mind off it. I found some places I thought worth looking at. Some rentals. Some condo's. Can we start looking tonight?"

"Sure."

Lacey smiled instantly, looked at her watch, then stood up. Not seeing anyone nearby, she leaned over and gave Tom a long kiss. "It's going to be fine. I'll make sure of it."

Trying to share in her exuberance he glanced through the stack and said, "These look pretty cool."

"I bet they're even better in person," she said, heading down the hall.

An hour later Tom settled into his routine and temporarily muzzled his thoughts about the night before. As he was looking over the prospectus for an oil and gas company, his phone rang. His display showed that it was the administrative assistant to Kent Jamison, the director of the department. Tom couldn't ignore the call.

"Hello, this is Tom Dabel"

"Good morning, Tom. I'm Miriam Taylor. Mr. Jamison would like to meet with you. Excuse the short notice but you're needed up there now."

"In his office?" he said, surprised at the request.

"No, in the Acropolis Room on 37. Do you know where that is?"

"No, but I'll find it. I'll be right up."

"I'll let them know you're on the way."

"Thank you."

Tom stopped first in the rest room to check whether he looked presentable. Thank goodness he didn't opt into the casual fashion of his coworkers.

He had noticed early on that management dressed formally in suits. He didn't wear a suit jacket, but he did take the middle of the road with a plain white shirt and tie.

It worried him as to why Mr. Jamison was calling him up. Did one of the companies he approved for investment go bankrupt? Did a misplaced decimal get past him? Will he be fired? Above all don't let his fatigue show. Be upbeat and just listen he told himself.

It was not hard to find. Two ornate cherry finished doors at the end of the corridor stood out from the light maple doors standard to the rest of the building. Once inside the waiting room he was greeted by a young associate. "Mr. Dabel? You can go on in."

The large meeting room was aptly named. The Greek theme was everywhere. Pictures of the Parthenon and other ancient antiquities hung on the side walls. Also against the walls were short stone Doric columns supporting glass cubes that held an assortment of objects. Probably courtesy gifts management received from business partners during their world travels. Two larger columns at the front framed a media wall for presentations.

"Take any seat," Kent directed.

Seated around the oval table were seven men and three women uniformed in black suits and bright colored ties. Tom recognized a few as department heads he had seen in the corporate newsletter. He surmised the rest were likewise executives. Most were young except the gentleman at the head of the table. He nodded to a red-headed man who made the introductions.

"Good morning Mr. Dabel. I imagine you might be bewildered as to why we summoned you here. My name is Olson and I am VP of Strategic Growth. In an hour we will be making some major announcements at the All Hands meeting. One is to expand our presence in global markets. More on that in the presentation.

"There will also be some restructuring causing a need for more leaders. To accomplish that we're kicking off a management development program called Pinnacle Path. This won't be part of the talk because only a select few will benefit. We have been watching you and see traits we're looking for -- skill with numbers, work ethic, judgement, team work. Other skills can be learned. Kent can review details with you later. Some aspects are still being created.

"To begin with, there is a set of level programs you will attend. You will be assigned a leader who will be your mentor, and you will receive cross-training through assignments in other departments, some for people in this room, others might be elsewhere.

"It's a lot to suddenly throw at you but that's the way this business works. We believe you have leadership material and can do it."

"Wow, this is a fantastic opportunity. I appreciate

that you selected me."

Olsen looked to the others. "Any questions from the group?"

For the next ten minutes, a few took turns asking about accounting and financial matters. They weren't particularly in depth. It appeared they were more interested in how he presented himself, not what he knew. Like his father often advised him, 'It's not what you say but how you say it that closes the deal'.

Olsen checked his watch then stood up. "Well, we have other duties before the meeting so time to close. Tom, thanks for coming up. You're free to go."

"Thank you so very much."

Nearly all of Tom's unit came to see the Braves that evening. They enjoyed a bird's eye view from the corporate skybox high above home plate. It was the sixth inning in the second game of a twilight double header. The team swept the first game with the Marlins but now trailed two to five.

Most of their attention was focused elsewhere since it was a chance to network. Tom was sitting with one group on the tiered seating discussing office gossip. Lacey was with another group refilling their plates at the well-stocked food bar.

"So I hear you and your lady are moving in together," Egan probed.

"That we are. As a matter of fact, we toured several condos with an agent before the game. Saw two we liked but we'll look again tomorrow."

"Got a target for moving in?"

"Yeh. We hope by the end of the month. It depends if we can pull off a contract and mortgage that quickly." Egan gave a doubtful look.

Riley Lirror, a co-worker from finance, sitting on the opposite side of Tom asked, "By the way, I heard you got called up by the big shots yesterday."

Tom wasn't prepared to elaborate on his selection to the Pinnacle Path program just yet. He had little details himself.

"Kent was there. It was a spur of the moment thing. He wanted me to fill in some details on something he was presenting to the executive committee."

"That's good for you. More visibility to top brass. It could lead to something bigger."

"Who knows?" Tom said dismissively.

Egan joined in again. "Say, if you don't mind my asking, how are things at home. Folks fine with your move?" Egan tended to delve into people's personal lives but Tom didn't mind. He was just trying to be a friend. Besides, it felt good to talk to someone about his challenges.

"No, they're not. In fact, they have been asking more of me lately. I don't mind helping out, but I was hoping when I told them they would give me some space. That hasn't been the case."

"I feel for you," Egan sympathized.

"Maybe when I actually move out they'll understand."

Lacey came back with two plates of dessert, motioned for Riley to move over and sat down beside Tom.

"What are you guys talking about that I should know?"

Suddenly the sound of the crack of a bat made them turn to see the play. The Braves second baseman hit a long fly ball that dropped in between center and right field. Two runs came in before the ball returned home. There was now a man on second and third with two out.

Tom's cell phone rang. The game was getting interesting and he wanted to return the call later. He saw it was his father though and answered it.

He listened, abruptly stood up and whispered in Lacey's ear.

"They just took grandma to the hospital! I have to go."

Tom drove across town back to Peachtree Corners to pick up his grandfather. Paloma had just brought him back from his appointment for new glasses. She had to remain at the house to watch her younger siblings. No one had been able to reach Altan.

They drove back into the city heading for Parker Medical Center. The senior Mr. Dabel was a quiet man, of a generation that did not verbalize any hurt or worry. He and his wife Anna had lived as simple nut and raisin farmers in Central Anatolia. When Emir became successful and they were physically unable to continue working the fields, they moved in with their children in Babek. Tom revered his grandparents and felt obligated to give them comfort.

"I didn't get much detail from dad. Apparently, she fell down the rear stairs going back to your place. It's only three steps, but she was carrying laundry and probably took the landing the wrong way. Parker is a great hospital. I'm sure she's getting the best care."

"My Anna has been kind of wobbly lately. Complained of dizziness. I think it's her eyesight. At 85, you have old eyes that don't see so well."

"Did you mention it to momma or dad?" Tom queried.

"No. She told me not to say anything. Did not want to impose on anyone."

"I'll say something to dad."

"I tell her over and over to get new glasses like me. But no. Stubborn. Just stubborn." he said, his voice shaking. Tom could not decipher whether he was angry or worried. "Please say something to Anna. She's very proud of you. When we call family back home, all she talks about is you. She will listen to whatever you say."

"It's not my place to press my babaanne what she should do. And mom and dad would be furious. I do care about you two so I may gently say something to her."

"Wonderful. I am sure it will help. I want to tell you something I would never say in front of the others," he said in a hushed tone, as if there was somebody else in the car.

"Of all the grandchildren, you're our favorite. You are a smart, handsome young man that brings dignity to the Dabel name," Munir confided, putting his hand on Tom's shoulder.

"Thank you, buyuk baba," Tom acknowledged with embarrassment. "I'm flattered, but you know we all love you -- equally."

"Yes. And the same for us. But you're special. The strength of the family will be in your hands as Emir and Irmek get older."

Ordinarily that would be a nice compliment to receive from his elder but to Tom it carried with it an impending burden he wasn't sure he wanted to bear.

"Thanks, again. And I'll be sure to say something to babaanna."

When they arrived at Parker Medical Center, Tom found a wheelchair for Munir so they could rush to Anna's room. Emir and Irmek came out so that the two grandparents could spend time alone.

"That took you a long time to get here," Emir grumbled.

"I had to go across town twice, and traffic was heavy," Tom answered. "So how bad is it?"

"Pretty bad. Broken ankle and a cracked hip. We'll

have to consult with the physician, but she'll probably undergo a couple surgeries and lots of therapy."

The family sat in the lounge discussing where in the house to move her when Munir came out thirty minutes later. His face was pale and walk shaky.

"Ziko, Anna would like to see you."

Upon entering, Tom saw her head was turned toward the window with her eyes closed. The company must have exhausted her so he hesitated in arousing her. Being the last for the day he decided to speak.

"Babaanna," he said softly.

She awoke and turned. When she saw it was Tom her eyes brightened.

"Ziko! Please come closer. I'm glad you came."

"I heard there was a party here so I came as fast as I could."

"I wish it were a party. I guess I'm getting too old to even walk around the house," She lamented. "Come closer, Ziko." She placed her frail hand on his cheek. "I don't know how much longer I'll be here."

"Don't say that! You'll be just fine," Tom said, redirecting the conversation before it got too depressing.

"I don't know. I'm a tired old lady."

"You're just sore now. And they're giving you medicine that makes you sleepy. The doctors and nurses will fix you up like new."

"I don't know. I hope so. It's all so strange."

Tom pulled up a guest chair close to the bed and

sat down. He listened as she reminisced about the old country. She missed Anatolia, the smells and tastes of the farm, and the family and neighbors she gossiped with every day. As much as Emir and Irmak tried to make Munir and her comfortable, she never felt at home. It started when they moved to Babek and grew worse in Atlanta. She felt out of place everywhere they went.

Tom felt a little uncomfortable but listened. This was an emotional subject that belonged between husband and wife. Serving as his grandmother's confidant made him nervous.

"I see in you everything that was good about Turkey. You are strong, handsome, smart. I hope you think about going back some day. Make it better."

He looked at her and smiled. There was no going back. At least not in the near future. The country Anna was experiencing in her mind did not exist anymore. And he was going to create his own bright future here.

"I know you have a girlfriend. She would love it in Istanbul if she ever had a chance to see it. Promise me you will think about it," she said, her eyelids closing.

"I'll think about it."

He slowly got up as she drifted into sleep.

Late that afternoon, Tom took a walk behind the house down to the Chattahoochee. Sitting on a downed tree, he listened to a musical prelude of natural sounds. A few birds were chirping their last chorus for the day giving way to the bullfrogs trumpeting the onset of evening. The sun had not fully set and rays of light penetrated the woods, polka dotting the embankment on the other side with coins of yellow.

Often, he came to this retreat hoping to sort through the conflicting demands he was experiencing. Or at least arrive at a peaceful acceptance that this was Tom Dabel's new normal. So far the river continued to flow past him with nothing to offer. He was just a bystander who was on his own.

If his parents would just cut him some slack. But as the purchase of a townhouse became more real, the appeals for his presence escalated. He didn't think it had so much to do with them needing help. At least not physically. They needed him to be the steward of their heritage. The more he connected with new friends and their way of living, the more upset they became that he was forsaking Turkey.

And Lacey was already making plans to redecorate and furnish the condo they selected, much of which would need his help. She was pressing for more of his time to troll the stores and participate in making selections.

Work too was more demanding. Late evenings had become the norm recently. He was part of an initiative to find funding alternatives for WorldTrust's global growth strategy. He expected the Pinnacle

Path training would ramp up soon too.

Lately, he had been coming to this spot more often, in search of a magic solution to integrate his mom, dad, Lacey, his friends and WorldTrust into a fulfilling life. He used to expect it would be the natural outcome of hard work and a friendly attitude. To be sure, multiple good fortunes did come his way, but not without conflicting consequences. It was beginning to look like it wasn't going to work at all and something had to give. What, he didn't know.

After an hour of fruitless analyzing, it grew dark and the mosquitoes took dominion over his refuge. He leaned forward, resting his head on his hands. With his fingertips he rubbed his temples hoping to stave off a headache. Some branches crackled behind him. Little Quiana was standing there, watching him.

With a puzzled look she asked, "Are you o.k?"

He got up and placed his arm around her shoulder. "Sure. I'm fine. I just needed a little time out."

"Good. Dad has been looking for you." Together they walked back to the house.

A month later, Tom was at the office, pouring over the final recommendation for the financial plan. Despite having two computers, his work area was buried in spreadsheets and ledgers. The regulars stopped by per their usual routine but he had to politely wave them off if he were to finish on time.

He and Lacey had just closed on their condo and

began painting the rooms before the new furniture arrived. Somehow he had to also find the time to get the utilities transferred to his name and have his address changed on numerous accounts.

His phone rang. He really wanted to keep working. Seeing it was Miriam he realized it was a call not to be ignored.

"Good morning, Tom Dabel here."

"Good morning, Tom. This is Miriam. Glad you're here. Mr. Jamison would like to see you."

"Did he say what the subject was?"

"No, just that he would like to see you now."

This time the meeting was not in the Acropolis room. It was in Kent Jamison's private suite on 28. Miriam greeted him when he arrived and motioned him into the office.

"Have a seat, Tom." His boss said in a slow, serious tone. A moment of pause then, "I wish I didn't have to say this. It's hard to find the words."

Tom's eyes widened and perspiration found immediate release. This sounded bad, very bad, Tom thought.

Kent could see Tom's state of alarm and laughed. "Not to worry. I can see I'm starting out wrong. I don't have bad news. It's like this. I had the management of global initiative come to me. They're desperate to fill a spot in their group. They want you. I hate to lose you, but it's a promotion."

"I don't know what to say," he replied while recovering but still surprised.

"We would rather have put you through the Pinnacle Path first. Instead it's ready, shoot, aim. That's how a lot of things get done here. Spur of the moment, turn on a dime."

Tom sat forward in his chair.

"They're starting a new territorial office with a rapid staffing requirement. You would be responsible for the financial component. This means learning on the fly. There are certain experiences you haven't had yet, but the executives see in you the talent and expertise they need. Whatever business acumen and political sensitivity you lack, they're confident you'll pick it up along the way."

"When would I start?"

"They prefer one week. I'm sure two will be ok."

"Where is it at?"

"Spain. Madrid, Spain."

Tom let out a small gasp followed by a couple of coughs to make it appear he was clearing his throat.

"Like some water?"

"No, I'm fine. Just a bout of allergies." He cleared his throat. "How long is the assignment?"

"Two years. It takes that long to establish a new office. Assuming the operation takes off, you may go to new countries, say China or Peru, as the business expands."

Tom was at a loss for words. Kent took note of his reticence.

"A word of advice: This is one of those once in a lifetime career opportunities. They never come back a second time to someone who passes up a promotion. If you succeed, there is no end to how far you can go."

"Hmmm," was Tom's only reply.

The sun had barely risen but the heat and humidity was already beginning to build. He was out on the water early with the goal of practicing his kayaking before the air turned brutal.

It felt great to be out here. For all the times he had come to a river's edge, he had never ventured out into open waters, at least not by himself. It was peaceful and beautiful, particularly the green cast of the Blue Nile. Most importantly, he was in control of where he was going.

It was a month since he left Atlanta. He wasn't able to picture a way forward. Everyone had a plan for him. His family wanted him to nurture and defend their roots. Lacey needed him to settle down and craft a household for the two. WorldTrust envisioned him as an executive recruit. They all meant well and sought the best for him. Trouble was they were plotting his course, not him.

And so he left it all behind. His rationale was that picking one facet of his life meant abandoning another. He would still be living in proximity to somebody in his circle he had to reject, which would hurt himself as much as them. Success was more likely with a whole new start, not half of one.

Once he decided to leave, he contacted an old college roommate, Alwarrikkibenlar Giduda from Ethiopia. Known as Ricky throughout the dorm, his friend never stopped extolling the virtues of his country and Tom determined it was as good a place as any to start anew. It was one of the safer regions in Africa, so Tom up and moved to Bahir Dar, a mid-sized city near Lake Tara and the Blue Nile. Ricky connected Tom with a local developer landing him a job keeping the books and paying the bills for the company. Being a small firm, Tom would occasional be expected to go onto construction sites and help the trades. Serving as their go-fer and learning a new skill sounded great to him.

Here he felt immersed in an evolutionary flow that matched his own. Parts of Africa were finally emerging out of their primitive cultures and leap-frogging their way to modern life. Like a gentrifying neighborhood in an old city, Bahir Dar was also joining the ranks of contemporary civilization. Condominiums, glass office buildings, trendy restaurants and movie theaters were springing up everywhere. Dirt paths were being replaced by paved roads. Cranes dotted the skyline. The country and the city were like him --- making decisions today that would define who they would be tomorrow.

And so, as the dawn began to brighten, he threw his effort into paddling against the green waters of the Blue Nile back to the landing near his apartment. Following a quick shower and getting dressed, he would be off to another fine day of work at Bright Horizon Enterprises.

ABOUT THE AUTHOR

Chuck First

Born in Cleveland Ohio, Chuck First graduated from Ohio University majoring in architecture and currently is an architect residing outside Richmond, Virginia.

BOOKS BY THIS AUTHOR

The Pegasus Tower

In this epic novel, an unbuilt design by Frank Lloyd Wright for a mile high tower is constructed by an international bank. This speculative fiction explores worklife in a mega-office which eventuall impacts the Seven Wonders of the World.

A Place To Be Happy: Linking Architecture And Positive Psychology

A guidebook for architects and interior designers on methods to utilitize the findings from a new branch of psychology to enhance the daily experience of office workers.